RAINY DAY TALES – VOLUME 1

I0456738

Edited by Dorothy Davies

RAINY DAY TALES – VOLUME 1

FICTION4ALL

TABLE OF CONTENTS

6

The Russian Doll Ban (SJ Townend)

Everyone remembers where they were, who they were with, on the day storing stuff inside stuff became outlawed. The *Trojan Invasion of Monkton* deflected all paths.

"I remember, Anuk. I wished to wait until you were older to help you understand. You're still so young, but my time is now. Let me share my story with you, as the last gift you will ever give me. Let me reminisce, for all I'll be shortly is a collection of memories. And once those memories cease to be relayed, I will cease to exist." Old man Rhiaj, riddled with fresh pain, pain which pin-balled through every inch of his dying body, searched his son Anuk's grey, limpid eyes for a neural connection.

"I apologise if this brings you discomfort, but it's better to understand than to live in ignorance. I hope some of my memories plant seeds within you which will grow into new fruit. How it has spun into where we are now, where I leave you today, I know not, but I know it's all wrong. Promise you'll look after your mother once I've passed. Take her underground."

A strong sun hung above Rhiaj, who was bleeding out. He was a collapsed heap on the blanket Anuk had thrown down after the attack.

An urbane skyscraper behind the two men partially interrupted the azure sky. The superstructure both reflected and transmitted the sun's rays in equal measure. It was the medical

7

centre from which Rhiaj had just been discharged. It had been built from transparent blocks, each of its wards, bays and waiting rooms could be seen from the street. The entire guts of the place were on display, as clear as day to those with good vision.

Every hospital gurney with patient atop lay physically separated from the street outside and from the other patients within, but each patient lay also exposed, dotted between glassy walls, suspended in a transparent tesseract of square cell on cell on cell. Cubist frogspawn.

In Rhiaj's side was a gash which fed blood to the gutter. From this unzipped₁ fresh tear hung strawberry shoelace lengths of artificial arteries and veins—plumbing—poking out, throbbing each moment with decreasing pace, dribbling vermillion.

"I will receive your story so I can share your history with my children. If I am blessed with finding the underground—if I am blessed with concealment and procreation."

"Lay on your hands, Anuk. It is time."

His father's words hung clarion in the space between them. Anuk closed his eyes, lifted his hands and put them on his father's temples.

As it pooled, history smouldered, embers hungry for oxygen in the eye of Rhiaj's mind. The old man's breathing quickened. He blew oxygen into his thoughts. A great fire grew. Rhiaj whipped up his many memories until they became a roaring cloud suspended between his temples. His memories danced down as luminescent tropical rain into and through the young boy's fingertips, along his arms. With the power of a million match strikes, energy and data charged along neurones, unlocking and lighting up the mind space behind Anuk's closed eyes with a fine and beautiful white light. This became a synergistic synaptic pinwheel of imagery, spinning and sharing, firing off and filing away things of significance and of the past in the recesses of Anuk's skull.

The boy held his hands in place until he could receive no more and the story was told and then he collapsed backwards, falling like a de-strung marionette into the road by which his father lay. His father winced and wailed in pain and became paler as the blood continued to leave his papery shell. The boy rose and returned to his father's side; older, wiser, yet still the same.

"I see you," the boy said after a timely pause, his skin whitewashed with exhaustion. "Thank you, Father."

The boy tried once more to stem the flow of blood with fabric remnants torn from the edge of the blanket, to no avail. "Father, don't go. I'll try and recover it. Or I'll search for the underground until I find the entrance and then I'll go below and seek one fresh; or one from an ox... or hands that can stitch and heal you. Let me lay down my hands once more and I'll receive direction. I believe you know where the underground can be found."

"No, child." The old man lifted his frail arm and cupped his son's chin in his hand. "I'm done."

The boy, his heart breaking, pushed his father's hand away, despite wanting to hold it tight to his face whilst it still pulsed, albeit weakly, with the juices of life. He wanted his father to cup his chin or

9

to embrace him wholly, to wrap him up in his arms more than anything he had ever wanted in his life. "You can't cup my chin, father. You can't conceal my jaw in your hand. We are exposed. The guards are volatile here. If one sees you with your hand on my chin, hiding it like you are, you'll be killed."

"I'm already dead, Anuk," Rhiaj replied. And with that, Rhiaj closed his eyes and exhaled a breath of one thousand wishes, a million could-have-beens.

***

CLARIFICATION AND EXPOSURE ACT, 2052

Part 1

Part 1 of this act makes provision about the capacity for clarity and exposure, in line with global policy.

All storage of goods, data, belongings, property, livestock, people and anything else as and when deemed necessary by the authority, is subject to the Clarification and Exposure Act (CEA).

Enforced application of the CEA protects individuals with regard to the dangers of concealment, in particular by—

Requiring all of the aforementioned items and any additional items as specified by law enforcers to be readily visible, exposed for communal clarity at all times.

Increasing visibility maintenance as a preventative measure in response to acts of terrorism.

Part 2

Part 2 (to follow) applies a broadly equivalent regime to certain types of storage to which the CEA does not apply. This shall include storage of government devices, government implements, government livestock, government employees, guests and those detained, data and belongings of those detained, and any other items as deemed necessary for law enforcement purposes such as storage of personal data and other items by Storage Services and the Storage Commissioner and the Crown and Parliament.

Of course, like every new piece of legislature, loop holes and caveats were written in for the elite, the government; civilians were provided with no access to Part 2 for scrutiny. No questions were asked. No questions were answered.

***

Policy had been trickling in for months before the day the legislation officially passed. Official edict had been relatively rapid with civil servants using the infrastructure already in existence from the Freedom of Information Act brought in fifty odd years earlier.

Changes had been subtle at first.

Sales of Tupperware boxes and transparent-backed smart tech such as mobile phones, televisions and handheld tablets had sky-rocketed in the lead up to the shaping of the new transparent world order. The construction of crystalline Perpsex multi-storey apartments had been well under way to prepare a substitute to opaque housing for the handful that could afford it. The many who couldn't slept fitfully in the run up to the day the law came into action, panicking and fretful about where they would live once the demolishment phase rolled out.

It hit harder than any other event of the millennia. Nine Eleven, the tragic loss of Diana, Queen of Hearts and the 2034 Submergence of Cornwall paled in comparison. Some liberals believed that government changes hit harder still than the initiating event, the Trojan Invasion of Monkton, or TIM day as it had been abbreviated to by the media.

TIM day. One thousand extremists had smuggled themselves into the vast storage units of a world-dominating, well known e-commerce and dispatch company. Three hundred trillion pounds worth of stock had been destroyed as the political extremists concealed within simple taped opaque cardboard boxes detonated themselves in the largest of the dispatch company's warehouses. A tsunami of international despair followed: people waiting weeks and months for next-day deliveries as a result of the global crisis. Rioting, piracy, violent crime and armed robbery escalated exponentially as the aggrieved needed and lusted for things which had suddenly become unavailable online. Supply and demand became a lopsided see-saw, tipping the planet into an existential capitalist nightmare.

***

On the morn of the day the global law was brought into play, by the break of dawn, the streets were littered thick with packaging and containers and other such suddenly illicit items.

A trail of detritus. Lidless jewellery boxes, clothing with rended pockets, smashed ceramic plant pots and brown glass medicine bottles, torn gunny sacks, kettles, trampled, boxy external hard drives, shredded plastic carrier bags, paper bags, flat screen televisions with their slim line backs cranked off, cracked vegetable waste caddies, fine leather bags in slices, new and dilapidated bags of all varieties in various states of destruction, chomped open tin cans, devoid of contents.

Like a tidal wash-up of plastic and metal, card and porcelain, ridded goods demarcated the edge of every block. Satellite maps showed litter trails that could be seen from nearly as far away as the moon.

By noon a graveyard of portable cupboards stood amidst the litter. Many had piles of coat hangers like funeral flowers lying by their side. Chests of drawers sawn into strips with anything burnable salvaged and piled up on resident's blankets could be found at the end of gardens. White goods with doors unhinged and salad crispers smashed to smithereens; joined the small fry.

In a world where from midnight past, cars, buses, taxis, any transport that involved hidden passengers had become outlawed. The police patrolled the street on foot or on horseback. They patrolled day and night in groups and anyone caught storing something inside of something else was immediately imprisoned.

The government think-tank had decided incarceration of lawbreakers in concealed prison blocks and bunkers was hypocritical so jail blocks constructed from invisi-fibre reinforced glass and Perspex had been erected months in advance in supermarket car parks up and down the country. The threat alone, the humiliation of being locked up outside in a transparent barred box for all to pass and see and laugh at had been enough to deter most from breaking the new legislation. But for those not deterred enough to eradicate all forms of storage and concealment from their professional and private lives, for those who chose to repeat offend, public execution was reintroduced.

Days rolled on and humans pushed the new firm boundaries. Bodies collected in piles and bodies were then lifted and carried to hill tops and tossed upon constantly burning funeral pyres. Coffins and urns, of course, were some of the first items to be destroyed. There was no greater concealment sin than storage of a body, be it dead or alive, within an opaque container.

Hanging, close range assassination and the electric chair were all brought back in with no time to debate the ethics or inhumane nature of each off-button device. The lethal injection had been outlawed as the powers that were deemed it an act of storage of stuff inside of stuff. Poison inside of flesh.

***

From the placing of hands, Anuk felt strong the memory of Rhiaj helping his Mother pull a sofa out through French doors and out on to the street on the day the law was brought in. They had dragged it as far as the pavement. Rhiaj's mother's back had given in. She had spent the rest of the afternoon wishing she could ice it as she lay on the sofa outside her home. Her discarded fridge, which sat perched on the kerb, swung wide its doored mouth, revealing an opened ice box, mocking her injury.

Anuk felt how Rhiaj had found it exciting at first—sleeping under the stars, a stone's throw from his former bedroom inside a house. The twins from his class, from down the street were homeless too. They had joined Rhiaj under the blanket of the night sky to share coverings of wool and cushions. They had shared a chicken meal. Mother had carefully cooked it by balancing it on the end of a pronged fork over the street barbecue.

Rhiaj recalled and passed to Anuk a memory of being snuggled in his sleeping bag and laughing, with the twins, who were of a similar age, with a similar silliness about them, at the guards in their Lycra. pocketless suits. The guards worked their way along the street applying crosses of red tape to every point of entry to every family home.

"When will this end?" Rhiaj had asked his mother. "When will we be able to return inside?"

She had said she didn't know, a few days perhaps, but he had known it would be longer. Something within him sensed he may never step foot back inside the place where he had grown up.

Anuk's fingertips sensed Rhiaj had felt safe at his mother's side as they toasted marshmallows over the barbecue. Each puffy mallow held and blackened in tongs under a bruised-navy night sky. Rhiaj had felt safe and strangely fine with it all, with the resilience or ignorance or both that children have. Fine, until the guards had shaken him awake at three or four in the morning, demanding he step out of his sleeping bag.

His mother received three lashes as she couldn't afford to pay the instant fine—she hadn't considered a sleeping bag would count as an item of concealment. Rhiaj felt his heart beat a little faster with new found fear as he watched the guards toss the zipped bag onto the street fire. It went up with unnatural blue and green flames and a chemical stench.

He had shivered until the morning came. He then walked with his mother for several miles over to her sister the other side of town to share a street pitch with them. There, Rhiaj passed time staring at a different house with the same red crossed tape stitching up the doors and windows. There, they shared a plethora of flat, two dimensional blankets with new neighbours as the nights tallied up.

He had missed seeing his own home blown into smithereens under controlled direction, but clearly remembered watching his aunt's three bedroom terrace sink down and in on itself; a mushroom of grey smoke and ash shooting up into the air above. He remembered the entire street becoming packed away, made transparent, invisible, folding into rubble and dust in an apocalyptic Mexican wave.

Rhiaj's mother and extended family could not afford a Perspex home. The majority couldn't. People improvised: gazebos, sideless shacks, rudimentary cities without walls were built, providing the minimum of protection and shelter necessary for survival, without breaking new laws. Through his father's shared memories, Anuk, sitting on the pavement with his hand's to his father's temples, saw all of this.

***

Anuk had matured through an era of great escalation. As the division between the uber rich and the rest of society widened into an expanse greater than that between two planets, many new rules were brought in.

Complicated clothing became outlawed, in the sake of enhancing visibility. Some chose to continue to wear see-through outfits: skirts with strategically placed zips, tops with strategically placed buttons, in some vain attempt to maintain decorum, but most could not afford the fashions and were left wondering and sleeping on streets in underwear made from the thinnest of cottons.

Shortly after Anuk had been born, the government decided that intercourse too was a form of concealment. Anything deemed to be going into or out from an opaque orifice was banned, no matter how long the concealment lasted.

It was at this point, that the rebellions rose and many moved underground.

Those storing themselves within caves were deemed Meta-outlaws by the extreme right who remained above ground, in their transparent towers.

Anuk—poor, above ground—knew no different than the life his father, Rhiaj and his mother had given him. They raised him under a large see-through awning pinned to a single wall, exposed substantially and adequately enough under the required clarity of the law. The sun became magnified as it fired down through the roof in summer. His eyes knew little of clothing or cardboard boxes or data sticks containing any form of information or books with their words hidden between front and back covers.

Each day posed the challenge of feeding and survival. Food needing harvesting from strips of crops that gave fruit above the ground only. Each collection of berries or seeds or nuts or pulses was only to be carried home for preparation on flat palms or in much-sought after clear borosilicate glass and high density polyethylene dishes and boxes.

***

Anuk's father, with age, needed life-saving surgery. Kidneys dropped in function, blood ran polluted. The family scrimped hard cleaning glass tenement windows and walls and toilets and baths and other such transparent property of the rich which filled the near-invisible landscape of the city.

Much toil occurred and Rhiaj received the donor transplant he needed. The procedure had passed without complications, despite the surgery falling under the umbrella of new government policy:

Section 4.3.1 amendment: a) Medical. Prohibited concealment of items is to be updated in line with world order to include medical devices to include: dental implants which burrow beneath the gum line, titanium joint replacements, transplanted organs, cardiac stents.

A donor kidney had been intricately connected to the new host, Rhiaj. Arteries and veins and nerves were stitched and entwined by robotic arms of surgical steel with great match, but then in line with government requirements, the wearing of the new donated organ was to be clear, visible. Rhiaj's entire smooth, brown kidney hung down, outside of his body in a transparent poly bag. Visible.

***

A societal change instigated by the poorly sewn seeds of terrorism had failed. With so much forced exposure, Rhiaj, like so many of those without— those who lived on the streets of flat blankets or under glassy lids held upright with poles—had learnt to hide away secrets.

Most precious memories became tucked away in the recesses of minds.

Hearts were worn on sleeves of skin. Those with little left to expose in the material world had learned how to harness innate telepathic communication with loved ones. They became able to share thoughts only with those they wished to share with. The ability to hide or reveal what had been stored away in the prison of the mind, the only place left for privacy, came fast.

The Exposure and Clarity Act had been set up to increase visibility, to prevent storage and secretive transport of items which could cause harm. But superfluous government policy ensued. Increasing the visibility of everything made those left with little more able to see the things they didn't have, which made them desire those items even more.

The youth on a semi-invisible scooter who'd sailed past Rhiaj didn't even need the organ that he'd yanked free from the old man.

The Bookshop (E. S. Sibbald)

The chime of the brass bell above the door seamlessly joined the melodic music filling the shop. The music, a mix of soft piano, violins and something akin to wind-chimes, sung from a grubby phonograph sitting on the counter beside an old-fashioned cash register covered with bronze levers and strange buttons.

Books with titles Celia had never even heard of filled the shelves, lined up like soldiers and piled in towers, leaning against each other like an extravagant house of cards. Most of their spines were cracked, frayed and in varying degrees of distress. Many were discoloured with stains and visibly fragile.

It was *exactly* the sort of place Celia had been searching for, something to make the trip with her mother to this boring little market town worth it.

Something rattled overhead and Celia tensed, gaze darting upwards to find herself looking at the underside of a toy train running across tracks strung from the ceiling to create the illusion they levitated. She followed it as it wove across the store, soaring over bookshelves, swerving around bends. There was little she could do to stop a smile from breaking across her face.

A shrill chirp sounded to her left and Celia tore her eyes from the train to find a small mechanical insect crawling joltingly across one of the many wooden shelves. She moved closer and could see it was not dissimilar to a stick insect, only crafted from glittering gold and had a body made of turning cogs and gears which groaned and clattered as the creature moved. Eventually, with a final shake, the cogs stopped turning and the creature stilled.

Celia pulled a book from one of the shelves. It was bound in blue fabric and had no title or author name printed on the cover. She flipped it over, there was no blurb either. Carefully, to avoid damaging the brittle yellowing paper, she opened the book and fanned out the pages. Neatly printed letters danced across her vision until midway through the book when they all turned blank.

Celia scrunched up her nose. Half the book was missing.

"Find something that interests you?" asked a silvery voice.

Celia spun to see an old man settling himself behind the previously deserted counter. He put a steaming cup of rich smelling coffee on a coaster beside the phonograph.

"Half the pages are blank."

The old man smiled, a glint of something that could have been mischief in his eyes. "Many stories have empty pages." He took a loud, leisurely slurp of his coffee. "Until they're finished that is."

That seemed obvious enough; nothing is ever created whole all at once, though it led Celia to another question. "Why would a bookshop sell unfinished books?"

The shop owner shrugged. "Every story deserves to be read by someone. Even the short ones, or the ones that no one ever finished writing."

"But who would bother reading only the start of a story?"

The man took another slow swallow of coffee and sighed. "You could make up the rest."

***

Celia walked out of the store; nameless book tucked under one arm. She sat down on a wooden bench outside, opened to the very first page and read:

The chime of the brass bell above the door seamlessly joined the melodic music that filled the shop...

There's Always a Stray Somewhere
(Rickey Rivers Jr.)

1.

The most selfish action in the world is to have children. Of course, I'm selfish as well, but I don't have children. I don't want them, not because of a particular hatred of them either. Children are fine. They're just little people after all, but plenty grow into worse versions of themselves.

When I speak on selfishness I mean lack of care. To bring a child into a world of suffering and pain is a heartless thing. Orphanages are full, of course they are, everyone's having children. It's the thing to do isn't it? You meet someone nice and plan a future. Funny how consideration of the child's future is never put into question, people don't care. It's "let's make a baby!" Like it's a pastry, something so simple, what could go wrong? Planning wrongness doesn't matter cause' you could just make another. But the pain of losing a child is heartbreaking. It would be difficult to consider another 'cake', as it were.

I remember the first time a woman asked me about children. It was awkward. We were six months into the relationship, all of a sudden here comes the child question. I nearly laughed in her face. I told her how I felt about children, saw her reaction. We broke up two weeks later.

I'm too old for fake companionship. It's something people crave, because it's a part of their biology, as if people can't reject what's inside. I reject so many thoughts every day, everybody does, those who don't go on shooting sprees. I don't envy the feeling of something snapping in your brain and that leading to attacks on the innocent. I reject that road, it's a weak one.

***

Work is pain, so is age, nearly every other day another body part hurts. Some of these seem like phantom pains, as in they feel so real that they become so, the location at times a ghost of a body part. Can't complain too much though, people don't like when others complain, much less men. Men have to shut up and bear the brunt of the world. Bear it so much you die, frail and broken down cause you worked so hard all your life. And why work hard anyway? What's the point, money? The same money people in power inherited? Then again, who am I to complain of anything? Inherited money was hard worked for money at some point, in some century, some back broken corpse is crying.

People don't like talking about that road. Everything comes from somewhere so all money came from somewhere, all of it can't be from 'hard work.' These jobs want to work you to the bone and don't you dare say it hurts, you bear that pain, you grin and you bear.

I've been at this new job for the past four months, done well too. Just moving junk from here to there, no drug stuff, warehouse work. Life's short though, thought about leaving but I left my last job too, so how many more jobs can I leave and still get work? Don't know. We'll see.

***

I used to work in an office, boring stuff with stuffy types. The best position was janitorial, those guys were cool. Feels weird calling stuff cool these days, but it's true. I respected the janitors. They didn't turn their noses up. I spoke to a few, had some good talks, they're just regular people with family and dreams.

At this office job I was sorting and developing software. Don't get too excited. The job consisted of sitting and more sitting and fake smiling and all the woes of office life. It's funny, though, some people love it. Those people kind of suck.

Even suck is a weird saying. I don't know. Language is constantly changing, not only from generation to generation, but also age to age. I don't sound how I sounded in my twenties. I hope I sound smarter than I was then, cause' I was pretty dumb.

Some would say I'm pretty dumb now for switching from an office to a warehouse job, but those people don't know me. So why should I care what they think? That's the kind of stuff you do when you seek companionship or friendship, constantly wanting approval, a ridiculous thing. I suppose an origin for my mindset is in order, but I reject the wanting. You're not owed anything.

Life is a series of disappointments. I've learned that over time, everyone learns that eventually if they live long enough. And who wants to live long anyway? That's such a cursed thing. Imagine being a vampire, having to live on and on forever. That's terrible. No wonder Dracula's considered horror. Immortality is a curse. To live forever is a death sentence.

I sometimes wish I were fictional. Then I could do some of the things in my head and not feel guilty. I wonder if other people feel that way. One woman freaked out when I mentioned that, shouldn't have probably. Definitely shouldn't have.

People tend to judge quickly. Thing is, I don't even blame them. Judge as harshly as you wish. I just don't like assumptions. People assume so much. I remember walking around the park this time and this woman with her kid and two other mothers kept looking in my direction. I guess they thought I was checking out the children. What morons.

Here's the thing about overprotective parents: you weren't protective enough not to have children. People looking at me like I'm some kind of sicko is hilarious, but whatever. People have their perceptions and their projections and you can't help projections, no matter how dim.

Don't confuse me. I'm not a child hating person. What I mean is, I don't inherently hate them. I hate that people don't take care of them, people who have them without thought, without care, without resources. People are stupid. You can't trust them to raise a small person. Plenty of folks can't raise animals. You ever see a dead dog or cat in the road? I have, I've seen plenty. Some folks purposely hit those animals too, much less raccoons and possums, not to say I care about the well-being of those

27

creatures either. They're in the same pack as children, no hatred.

Now, what do I care about? I like reading, information is nice. That's the best thing about the internet. No, it was the best thing, before people started sucking themselves completely into devices, a sort of digital fellatio. Nobody cares because they're satisfied and their souls are being sucked every day. It's a want. Then it's a need.

Another apparent need is children. We all need something to love. Children are not things but are treated as such, little toy things we can hold and dress up. So many women treat them like pets, ironically those without treat pets like children, same box creatures.

***

If a person had a choice, would they choose to be here? I think about that when I think about children. I wouldn't want mine to suffer. It's interesting having the choice to go out your own way. People don't like that, they think it's selfish, but everything you do in life is. Get over it. You have to, what else can you do when a person is gone? There are no BS conversations to go through when you're dead, you're just dead.

I don't like talking about death. I already think about it enough, it's just funny how folks love taking choices away from you in life. You can't even choose the way you want to die. If a loved one told you how they'd like to go out you might look at them funny. Truth is their choice is important. A person should always have it. My decision is a choice, one my parents refused me.

Speaking of them, they weren't as clichéd as suicidal thoughts. My father met my mother in school. They lost contact for years, then linked up again and finally got serious after my mother was so kind as to visit my father seeing his mother in the hospital. Dad said she was the kindest woman, did more even when you wanted less. She wanted to be there with him, even when Grandma passed Mom sat with Dad and just held his hand.

After that, Dad kept contact with her, sealed the deal, said he loved her and she him. I wonder if they thought about me after Grandma left. They say one life lost bears another life soon or something like that.

I think about Mom and Dad together sometimes when I'm standing somewhere high. I think about their disappointment with me. It's weird to feel you've failed your parents. It's not an intentional failure. They say life is a gift, but people reject gifts all the time.

I can't pretend I haven't had good moments in life, but life isn't just that, not that it needs to be. I'm not sure what it needs to be. I'm just sure that I've been dissatisfied and confused. Joys in life don't take away thoughts of ending it.

Sorry, Mom and Dad, you were good parents. You don't deserve me leaving how I want to leave, but it'll be my choice.

2.

Currently I'm driving, who cares where. My ride along is a handgun in the passenger seat. Quit work, no warning, spontaneous is the way, but it's not spontaneous, is it?

I didn't want to be discovered at home or work or anywhere where someone who knows me could find me. So I'm driving nowhere to find wherever. Got the gun weeks back, thought about my decision a while, my mind didn't waver. As straight as a winding road is the choice and all I can think of is the destination, not the location, but the destination after there is no noise.

Out the corner of my eye I pass by someone standing on the side of the road. It's a kid, a little boy with a backpack. He's got his thumb out, must be a trick. Still, something inside says to slow down and I do and I stop and what am I doing, a good deed before dying? Sure, why not?

The boy comes to the passenger side, as quick as can I put the gun into the glove compartment and unlock the door.

"Hello," he says.

I say hello.

The kid steps in.

***

There's a kid in the passenger seat of my car on the same day I'm supposed to do the ultimate deed. What am I doing?

The kid is quiet. So quiet it makes me uncomfortable. I say something to ease myself.

"Where can I take you?"

"Doesn't matter," he says, "just away."

I shake my head and slow down the car. The kid's eyes get big. "What are you doing?"

I tell him I need somewhere to take him, otherwise I'll have to kick him out.

"Just drive," he says. "I don't wanna go home."

I look at the kid's face. When he says home, his eyes look sad. Somebody should do something, somebody not me, somebody who's not supposed to die today. I say nothing. I drive on.

***

After some time a plan comes to me. "I'll take you to the police. They'll figure things out."

"No they won't. The police suck! I've called them before."

At this point I'm annoyed. "Called them about what? Tell me something so I know what to do."

"Just drive!" He says. "You're a driver, right?"

My eyes go from the road to the kid and back again. What happened to him?

"What's your name?" I say.

"Does it matter?" he says.

"Okay, I'll call you difficult."

"Fine by me," he says, folding his arms. "You can put it on my grave."

I tell the kid not to joke like that.

"Who's joking?" he says.

I say nothing. Soon I pull into a gas station and tell the kid to stay put. Don't know why I said that, seemed responsible.

"Bag of chips," he says.

I shut the door.

The whole time from inside to outside and getting the gas my mind was moving fast. I didn't know why I put myself in that situation. All I had to do was find a nice place and pull the trigger. Why'd I have to pick the kid up? I can't even answer myself.

Back inside I give the kid his bag of chips.

"You like those?"

"Yeah, don't matter, just needed some salt."

I say nothing and pull off.

After the kid finishes his chips he looks at me for a while. Then he blurts out what should have been lying next to me.

"Why do you have a gun?"

Now I'm stuttering. "W-what-"

The kid laughs. "It's cool, man. I've seen guns before."

"How old are you?" I say and the kid turns away. He looks out the passenger window and says fourteen.

"Okay," I say, finally information. "Are you ready to tell me your name?"

"Look, man," the kid says, and starts pulling up his shirt.

I stop the car, turn my head and wave my hand for him to stop.

"Just look," he says.

I see that his stomach and chest are bruised up. He turns around, his back is worse.

"So, that's what home is like."

"Yeah," he says. "Home is hell."

"Your dad?"

"Mom and Dad, but Mom doesn't hit like Dad."

I grip the steering wheel, remind myself to breathe. "You ever think about foster care?"

"Sure, I thought about it," he says. "I thought about a lot of stuff. I thought about killing myself too."

I raise my hand to him, as non-threatening as I can. "Don't say that."

And he looks like he's about to talk back, but I guess he saw what was in my eyes and pulled his words in. I had to soften my face to speak further, didn't want him afraid of me.

"You gotta find help, it just can't be me."

"Why not?" he says, "you picked me up."

"Yeah, I did." I drive on.

We're on like that for a while. The kid tells me about himself, talks about school, about video games, music and fights with teachers. Says he tried reporting his parents before but the police took their side because his dad knows someone in the department. So they wouldn't let anyone take him away from his folks. The whole time all of this is making me feel anger, hatred.

The sun sets over the horizon.

***

"Getting late," I say. "We should find a place to stay."

He says, "We can sleep in the woods."

I think about it, kid probably doesn't want a strange man taking him to a motel. Makes sense, we don't know each other.

"Yeah," I say. "That's probably safe."

"Or just park the car somewhere. I'll get out."

"What?"

"Yeah, we're far enough away from my house now. I can find a place for the night."

I think about it and agree.

I park the car close to a wooded area with a steakhouse on the other side and some train tracks to the left.

"Cool," says the kid, "find a place to stay and meet me tomorrow. I'll be in this area."

"What?" I say. "What's the point of that?"

Kid says, "Just do it."

With that the passenger's side door is closed and the kid walks out of my life. What a mess. What a big mess.

3.

I set myself up in a dingy motel room for the night and think how the kid probably got the better deal. I should have got the room for him and slept on the train tracks. I'm lying here staring at the off white colored ceiling and thinking about where life can bring you even if you're not prepared for it. I think about how many people probably had sex in this bed, about how many people probably died in this bed, probably killed themselves too and I probably should get the show on the road.

I leave the room and head into the parking lot. I go to the passenger side and open the glove compartment. The gun's gone. Of course it is.

Now I'm angry and pacing around the car. I actually look under the car, but I knew what happened. I just wanted to remind myself I was still stupid. I went back to the motel room and splashed some water on my face, it had a weird taste. I look in the cracked motel room mirror. What have I gotten myself into?

**

The night wasn't as bad as I thought it might have been. I slept about four hours, watched infomercials then slept for three more hours. I was hungry, less angry. I thought about the kid and went on my way.

It didn't take long to get back to the steakhouse area. I sat there awhile looking at the train tracks. Some early birds were already up and driving on their way to work or wherever. Whole time I'm thinking I shouldn't be here.

The kid sneaks up on me and opens the passenger's side door.

"What's up?" he says.

I make my face say the words before me. "Where's my gun?"

He smiles.

I don't.

"I wanted to practice."

I close my eyes and exhale. "Give it here."

The kid reaches into his bag and pulls out the gun. "Sorry."

I snatch it and toss it to the backseat.

"You're mad!" he says.

35

"What do you think?"

"I just wanted to have some fun with it."

"Fun with a gun," I say.

He smiles. "Yeah, I never used one before."

"And you had to take mine?"

"I'm fourteen."

"That's not the point!"

My tone made the kid push himself against the passenger side door. I was breathing hard, my hands were shaking. "The gun was mine. I needed the gun."

"I gave it back."

"I needed it yesterday."

"For what?"

Stupid kid, I point to myself. He laughs.

"What's funny?"

"You were gonna kill yourself? You told me not to."

I shake my head.

"Do as I say, not as I do? Just like Dad."

This upset me. I look into the kid's face. He's hurt, of course he is. He doesn't understand why the stranger reminds him of his father. It's because I'm a man and he's confused kindness with the idea of anger, as if anger can't come from all kinds.

"Kid," I say, "Don't compare me with your father."

"Then stop talking like him."

I stick out my hand, an open hand, a kind hand. "Okay, just tell me your name."

The kid puts his hand in mine and shakes it. His hand is small but callused, he's a worker. He's dealt with tools before. Life has taught him how to grip another man's hand. He smiles at me and says his name, "Wilt."

"Okay," I say. "I'll call you that."

***

After breakfast we talk some more. Wilt says he was thinking about his parents the whole time he had the gun, said he thought about going back home and shooting them both. I said I didn't blame him, but he shouldn't do every thought that came to his head. He asked me if I ever did and I didn't wanna lie to him because it seemed like he was starting to trust me. I said I sometimes did the thoughts in my head, but I knew they weren't good thoughts. They were thoughts that would make me feel better and that included carrying the gun with me on the road.

Wilt apologized again for taking the gun. I said it was okay. It really wasn't though. I was still upset with him, but didn't want to directly show it. Wilt was still fourteen and had just left a terrible situation. Why would I show him anger now, even if he deserved it? Who cares what we deserve anyway?

***

Wilt gave me more information on his abuse. Told me about the time his mom was called from school and she waited for him to get home so she could sit on him and tear up his back. I hated that. I hated every horrible thing he told me. At one point he stopped talking and stared outside the driver's side window. A dog was limping nearby and sniffing the ground.

Wilt left the car and went to the dog with his takeout box of food. They were out there a bit. Wilt gave the dog a sausage and petted him, looked like he was saying something to him too. I hoped he wouldn't want to keep it, seemed sick, on his way out.

Wilt ate something out of his takeout box and left the rest for the dog. Then he petted the dog a bit and came back to the car.

"Nice dog," I say.

"Yeah, he's cool, looks like somebody use to have her."

"How can you tell?" I say.

"She looks clean, but beaten. She's sick now."

"Yeah," I say. Then think. "You want her?"

Wilt laughs. "Nah, she'll be dead soon. She can have the fast food."

***

Back on the road and a question has been stuck in my mind for some time. It's a question that doesn't make sense for a rational man to have, yet I have the question bouncing around the inside of my head like a bullet without a place. It's an unreasonable ask, but I ask all the same.

"Wilt," I say. "Do you actually want to kill your parents?"

"Of course," he says. No thoughts to it, no further consideration, just a plain fourteen year old answer. So flippant it hurts.

I stare out the windshield at the road ahead. We're so far away from either of our homes it wouldn't make sense to turn around. So why did I ask that question? Because I'm angry, I'm still angry after Wilt stops talking about every punch, slap, dig, push and kick. I still want to use the gun because I never got the chance to use it. All of this is banging around my head when Wilt stops my thoughts and asks me a question, one that's probably been on his mind for a while.

"You ever kill anyone?"

"No," I say and that's true, never had the desire to take anyone out but myself.

I ask him the same question and he says nothing. I turn to him and his face is stuck, he's thinking. Why's he thinking so hard?

"Wilt," I say. "You ever killed anyone?"

"Not on purpose," he says and I'm almost surprised.

"I was practicing, didn't mean to hit nobody."

"Of course," I say, "of course."

It's quiet for a while then Wilt says "I didn't know he was there."

And I shush him, for some otherworldly reason I shush the child in my passenger's seat. I shush him so soft I surprise myself. And we're quiet for a while just driving this road and going nowhere. And he again breaks the silence and says, "Do you still want to die?"

And I'm thinking so much, about life, about this boy; how he had a home he ran away from, how the adults in his life failed him. And I'm considering options and I'm thinking terrible things and I'm pressing the gas and Wilt grabs the wheel and pulls me back from my drifting and he's screaming "Watch the road!"

And I do and I'm almost shocked when I see I can scare a person with inaction. A big horn blows. A transfer truck zooms by. Then I brake hard. I shift to park. I twist the key and stare out the windshield. I'm shaking.

I can't even turn to Wilt before he's grabbing me by the shoulders and calling me stupid. I push away and I see that he's crying, so I pull him close and squeeze him tight. I don't think about the marks on his back. How they'd probably hurt if I hugged him too tight. I don't care. I just hug him.

"Not fair," he says.

And he's hugging so tight and crying and calling me stupid and I think about the gun and it's just there and what would happen if someone found us dead in the car with a gun and our bodies mangled in a wreck?

The responsibility of taking care of another person: how stressful it is. And is it all worth it to live for a simple act like receiving a hug from another person, a person you don't know, but a person you might care for, if only for a bit, for as long as you both live?

"Not fair," he says.

And we could die together, yes. But we could also cry together laugh and live together for as long as we're allowed. And allowed is the right word choice. It is.

I apologize to Wilt and he's still hugging me like I would leave him. Deep down I believe he thinks I will, but I'm willing to prove him wrong.

Birds on a Wire (Rie Sheridan Rose)

When I was a girl, I would see birds on the telephone wires or electrical grid and think, "My sisters and I are like those birds. Grouped together in solidarity and companionship." It was a pleasant thought.

We grew up, of course, and things changed. I watched the birds split up and regroup and the metaphor still seemed apt—we went our separate ways: to school, to marriage, to employment... but we would still come together for family events.

Like funerals.

I stand here, looking around the chapel and the analogy feels even more apt. A bunch of us stand around in our finest black feathers and pretend we're a group. We pretend our nest is still the old homestead, now that the heart of it is lying in the coffin at the front of the room.

Mother was always the heart of the house. Papa stands to one side of the casket—lost, shrunken, and gray—when did he get old? For that matter, when did I?

I shake the proffered hands and bill and coo answers to the soft condolences like a dove in a tree, hiding from the others. I don't want to share my grief. It is mine and I have so little that is completely mine.

My second husband comes up and murmurs softly, "She was a lovely woman."

"Yes, yes, she was," I reply—wondering where my current husband is. He's supposed to be beside me, isn't he? At a time like this. Thank God, the first didn't decide to make an appearance.

My eldest sister catches my eye from across the room and starts over. I panic. I don't want to speak to her... not now.

A surge of raw, wild anger and grief surges up in my breast, so sudden and violent I almost double over. That would never do.

Instead, I turn and flee for the courtyard. The church has a lovely atrium and I barely stop myself from running to reach it. Outside, I try deep steadying breaths, but only manage to restart the tears which have been flowing off and on since the phone-call three days earlier that led to this pass.

I sob, wrenching, wracking, tearing sobs that sound like a monkey howling at the moon. Too whiny for a wolf.

I feel a hand on my arm, and realize I'm not the only one to take advantage of this hiding place. My youngest sister pats my arm. She smells of patchouli and perhaps a hint of cannabis. Her broomstick skirt sways around her like ebon wings as she hugs me. "It'll be all right. It'll be all right."

I rear back. "How can anything be all right again? She's dead!"

"But we're not. We have to carry on. We have to be strong."

"You be strong—you all be strong. With your families to nurture and your children to raise and your jobs to pursue. And I will be me. Falling apart at the seams."

The sympathy in her eyes makes me want to peck them out.

The others find us now and, for a moment, we are back in the nest—a huddle of togetherness before we all flew our separate ways. Brought together by time and circumstances we hoped would not come in our lifetimes, but were inevitable, really.

Birds on a wire may look disparate and alone, but they are bound by tradition and ties to wheel away, only to return. Family is stronger than we wish to acknowledge in times of despair. And no bird soars alone forever.

Coral's Call (Olivia Arieti)

Long red hair, green eyes and a pearlescent carnation would have made of Coral the perfect mermaid if the most beautiful legs hadn't belonged to her as well. Her hometown was an isolated fishing village on the north coast with lonely stretches of sandy shores and the steepest cliffs. The sea lured her and, besides spending her time watching the waves die on the shore, she was intrigued by the stories, mainly legends and folklore, where the sea and its marine dwellers were the protagonists. More than once her imagination led her to the most absurd assumptions; her father was a fisherman and couldn't he had fallen in love with a selkie who, after regaining possession of her skin, returned to the depths of the ocean? Her mother's premature death a few days after her birth alimented the fantasy. Whenever she asked about her, the rugged face darkened and she was begged not to renew the pain. Was that his way of concealing the truth?

She recalled how once a gorgeous lady, surrounded by a faint glimmer, approached her. The green eyes were glittering with joy, the smile, tender. She gave Coral big, coloured shells and before the child could say anything, ran away. Shortly afterwards, she caught sight of a dark mass bobbing above the waves and watched it rapidly disappear into the blue surface.

Could it have been an hallucination due to the many hours spent under the sun? The shells were still there though, a precious gift Coral would always treasure.

After her father's death, she left the village and moved to the city where a promising career as an interior designer waited for her.

Adjustment hadn't been easy; the fastidious hustle and bustle had replaced the quiet of her beaches, the magnificence of her cliffs.

She felt as though she had become a different person. Her new self was ambitious, tense, always under pressure with no time for dreams or fantasies.

Also, her child supposition made her laugh; her only regret was not telling her father about it.

Sean, whose firm was renowned for designing and decorating holiday homes, helped her out. The architect had spotted her talent and was eager to mentor her; soon his mentorship turned into courtship.

Coral had something about her that totally enticed him while up to now, his main concerns were making money and slipping into the beds of the many girls hopeful to tie the knot with the booming and wealthy bachelor; he began considering the eventuality of settling down.

After work he showed her around the city, took her to exclusive restaurants and introduced her to his snobbish friends who couldn't understand how such a refined and high class gentleman could fall for a simple, lowly girl. His father also disapproved and hoped he would soon get over it.

The young man, though, opposed all diffidence and difficulties with even more stubbornness and resolved to propose.

The occasion was given when a client wanted to restructure his old villa by the sea. Sean and his apprentice were supposed to take care of the project.

The keys were in his pocket along with the emerald ring when he jumped into his convertible with Coral by his side. Her satin green dress matched her eyes and her legs were a continuous distraction for the driver. He pulled over the car and was about to take out the ring when her detached glance made him quickly withdraw his hand.

"A penny for your thoughts, honey."

"Simply thinking of home, of my dad mending the nets, of the beach I used to walk along…" and sighed, "it all seems so far away… if not lost."

"What nonsense, dear, you can go there whenever you want."

"It wouldn't be the same," she replied nostalgically.

Although decayed, the villa still retained its past splendour. It was almost a pity to turn it into a modern structure and demolish the turrets, the big terrace; the majestic staircase. They realised there was a lot of work to do and while Sean would consider the structural design at the studio, Carol would spend some time there to live the house and better understand what kind of indoor and outdoor furniture and decorations were needed to modernise it.

After dining at a nearby restaurant, they lingered on the terrace for a drink. The full moon, the starry sky and the wind whispering discreetly made the atmosphere perfect to propose.

Sean's unfamiliarity with such a step was evident when he took out the little box and muttered, "I love you, Coral, never thought I could love a girl so much but it happened and now I want you to become my wife."

The gem sparkled before her.

Coral gazed at him, "This is so sudden ... I don't know what to say…"

In a flash her future unfurled before her; it appeared brilliant, successful and even glamorous. She would be happy… or at least learn to be… After all, she did like Sean even if she wasn't in love with him.

Plans for the wedding followed and, after draining champagne to begin the celebrations, they went upstairs.

Sean glanced at her alluringly, "No reason to wait for the first night, sweetie," he whispered and slid down the straps of her laced nightgown. Then he took her arm and was about to pull her down on the bed, when as though fighting a sudden battle between pure love and lewd desire, he warned, "I demand a lot, baby."

She realised that, even if unconsciously, he would always consider her his humble subject.

After a quick glance at the precious jewel that apparently, sparkled even more, Coral got into the bed.

The owner wanted the house to be ready for the following summer and since it was late winter, the works had to speed up and the wedding postponed.

Coral didn't mind; she was glad to have the chance to go back there and spend some time alone. Despite the amount of work, she managed to take strolls by the sea or visit the picturesque fishing village that somehow resembled her own,

On a morning unusually warm, she took off her shoes and walked barefoot on the shore.

"Don't you think it's a bit too early to put your feet in the water?"

She turned round. Before her stood a brawny guy with a tanned face and dishevelled blond hair; a few wrinkles were visible despite the young age.

"I'm Brandon, one of the village's fishermen. You must be the lady dwelling at old Rawson's place."

"That's me, Coral Lanes."

"Say, you don't look like a posh city girl. Where're you from?"

She told him her story, how she ended up in the big city and was about to get married.

"Too bad, baby, you'd have made a great fisherman's wife," he remarked quite abruptly and walked away. That night Brandon's face replaced Sean's. She couldn't get him off her mind... also his roughness was attractive... much more than the sleek refinement of the city gentlemen.

She was eager to see him again and she did.

"Have you ever took a dip at this time of the year?" he asked, almost provocatively.

"Never," she laughed, "not too fond on freezing."

That morning Brandon told her about himself, of his sea adventures and how a sudden storm destroyed his old boat, there only remained the wooden wreck that kept him adrift.

"It's been hard to get on my feet again, but here I am. Now I have a new boat," and he chuckled. "Only a wife is missing."

Then he gently moved back her hair and said, "Say, you look like a mermaid, doll, has anybody ever told you?"

"What if I told you my mom was a selkie instead?"

"No problem, I might be a selkie's son as well. Someone did save me from drowning before I got hold of the wreck."

Coral frowned; sure he was making fun of her.

At the weekend, she had to go back to the city. Sean had arranged the party to announce the wedding.

"Hey, you seem tired, hon," he said on meeting her at the station.

"Been working hard lately and there's still a lot to do," she replied as Brandon's image flashed before her.

"I'll let you relax this afternoon, but not tonight," he said and smiled. "I'm planning to surprise you, bought some toys for naughty girls."

The word *naughty* disturbed her. She had already become a very bad girl in her dreams and knew she wouldn't resist temptation for long.

The reception was fabulous; his father had finally given in and, although reluctantly, his well-off guests couldn't do anything but welcome her aboard.

Coral was unhappy and longed to go back to the fishing village.

When she returned, Brandon was on the beach, waiting for her.

"Did you get married? he asked.

"Not yet, but I'm getting close to it," she replied gloomily.

"Well, it's warmer now, what about that swim?"

"Why not?" Coral brightened up and took off her shoes.

"You have to do better than that, doll," Brandon said while unbuttoning his shirt and smiled, "if you prefer, I'll turn round."

When she was ready, they jumped into the cold water; expectation had fuelled desire and desire made them feverish; their febrile bodies clung together and finally their lips touched and their hands searched with the ardour of a first time encounter.

"You smell like the ocean, baby, you belong to it, like me."

Suddenly, a dark figure appeared in the distance, as though riding the waves.

"What's that?" she cried, frightened.

"A sea creature, you should know the sea is their home," replied Brandon calmly.

Once in their clothes again, he turned, worried, sad.

"Are you sure you want to give a kick to wealth and success? I can offer nothing more than a quiet life, with scrapping kids perhaps and a modest house."

51

His voice was adamant, his offer not negotiable.

"I'll talk to Sean, darling."

She did belong to the sea, but also to Brandon; the call had reached her and she had to respond.

Somehow rumours always have their way of sneaking through and reached the well-off friends. The romance of the lovely designer with a brawny fisherman had become daily gossip.

Fury seized Sean who promised revenge. He cried like a spoilt child whose favourite toy had been taken away and cursed like a man who had been basely offended. The sting of such an offence prevailed on his love. Coral had made a fool of him before everyone and had to pay for it.

When she arrived with the intent to settle the matter and give him back the ring, he was calm and affable, fearful that his wicked plan might go astray.

"There's a beautiful new boat waiting for us at the harbour, my dad's present. I want to show it to you and take you for a ride, honey."

"First we have to talk, Sean."

"We can talk during the ride," she said and headed towards the port. "The weather's not good and the sea's quite rough."

"No worry, baby, I'm an excellent skipper," he replied before starting the powerful engine.

Cold gusts and spurts of water hit Coral's face.

"Where are you heading?" she cried.

"Towards the middle of the sea, want to meet your fisherman, doll," he laughed raucously.

Then he stopped the engine and, with bloodshot eyes, grabbed her arm. "So you wanted to make me appear ridiculous, stupid, you bitch, thought you'd get away with it, but you won't," he shouted, took out a pair of handcuffs and quickly locked them around her wrists.

"You know how much I like these toys, how punishment diverts me," and with all his might he pushed her out of the boat.

A dark figure instantly rose from the water and lifted the vessel, making Sean fall out. Then it dived back, got hold of Coral and slowly dragged her to the shore.

The girl managed to open her eyes just in time to fix them into the marine creature's eyes; they were the same as the mysterious lady who gave her the shells... as green and human as hers.

"Mother," she muttered, but once again the figure had vanished.

Nobody could ever explain what happened to Sean or how a handcuffed person had reached the shore except Brandon, who never doubted his bride's-to-be words.

All Down The Lonely Years (Dorothy Davies)

Charles Grey walked slowly toward the school, arms swinging loosely in the disjointed shambling walk the old sometimes assume. The sun silvered the thick tight curls clustered around the bald patch, a halo of unconventional colour. The pavements were hot; his old shoes were no protection against bubbling tar. Already his tie felt as if it were confining his throat and pulling the collar into his neck.

He was almost there. Soon he would turn the corner by the old Oxfam shop, blank-faced and dusty, and then he would be able to see the stone wall surrounding the playground, topped with multi-coloured heads calling greetings to those approaching, yelling goodbyes to those departing. Same every day. Didn't they ever tire of it?

"Hello, Mr. Grey!" Children ran to his side, catching hold of his hands, spilling talk and laughter as easily as the sun slid through the branches of the sturdy oak shading one playground corner. He listened to the excited talk until he reached the door, then he paused for a moment to allow the children to drop back and let him enter the coolness of the corridor. He blinked in the shade suddenly imposed on his old eyes and found his way to the classroom by instinct.

The heat was stifling. He opened the windows and the door leading to the courtyard at the back, to let some of the slight hot breeze move through the chalk and schoolbook dusty room. He rearranged the papers on his desk, looking up only when he heard the bell, calling the children into pushing jostling lines ready to file into class.

And morning lessons began.

In the staff room at break time he drank tea, listened to teacher gossip complaining about classes or muttering about the Head's new rules, but he wasn't really listening, just letting the talk drift over his head. It was so hot he almost wished it was his turn for playground duty so he could walk outside. But that would have meant treading the hot asphalt and children holding on with sweaty hands. Perhaps it was better to stand at the window and feel the breeze touching his face.

Lunchtime was the rest period. He would leave the school and walk narrow country lanes, staring out across deserted fields, burning and cracking open in the heat. His bald patch turned red under the sun's rays and he wished he had some kind of hat. An hour was just long enough to stroll, to pick a long grass to chew, to listen to the birds and insects, before making his way back for his favourite afternoon session, English, and story time to finish the day. It was everything he wanted out of life. He would let the rich language roll from his tongue and even if it did go over the heads of some of the children, they savoured the sound and feel of the writers –

"Who knew their craft, by God!" he would announce in the staff room, knowing even as he did so that he was adding another layer to his reputation as an old fogey. It didn't matter. The children loved it and so did he. The school could go take a running jump at itself if it thought he would give up his story time for anyone!

When the reluctant hands of the clock finally touched 3.15, the children poured, shouting, into the playground to find their waiting mothers. The school would sigh with relief as the last pounding feet left the corridors to settle in dust and silence for the night.

Charles Grey walked alone round the school, touching dust-covered desks, disturbing a pile of books precariously balanced these long, lonely years and a single tear escaped to run unheeded down his face. How long had he been coming here, day after day, acting out the ritual of teaching a class full of children who longer came, children who now sat at home before the all-powerful, infallible screen?

"Damn the things to hell! he thought savagely.

"Hey Mister, what're you doing here?"

The black hair flopped down over the button bright eyes of the boy who stared at him. Charles stared back. He had heard no sound; the boy had appeared as if by magic.

"I could ask – what are *you* doing here?"

"My telescreen's broke; I came out for something to do."

"I'm remembering what it was like to teach here."

The boy perched on the edge of a desk, tipping the legs off the ground. Charles closed his throat on the sharp words before they left his mouth. It wasn't his school any longer; he had no more right to be here than the boy.

"What's that?" asked the boy, after very carefully scrutinising Charles.

"What's what?"

"Teach – whatever you said."

"Your telescreen shows you how to do things, doesn't it? How to write, draw, add up?"

"That's right."

"I used to do all that here, with a lot of children."

"Does that mean you know as much as the telescreen?"

Charles laughed. "Well, not as much as your telescreen, perhaps, but I knew enough to teach the children."

"My name's Terry." In a sudden burst of friendliness and trust the boy thrust out a grubby hand and Charles took it without a flicker of hesitation.

"I'm Charles."

The bond of friendship was sealed in that moment. Charles looked into the open face; the smile spangled with freckles and felt his heart turn over. This would make pretence even harder, knowing there were still bright-eyed boys around who were curious enough to come looking in the old school.

"What was it like?" asked Terry, looking around at the inches-thick dust encrusted on everything. "And why is that desk the only clean one?"

Charles smiled, a little self-consciously. "Play-acting at my age needs props. I use the desk when I'm pretending to teach."

"Were all these desks for the children?" Terry counted them, his eyes wide with astonishment. "Twenty-five? Were there twenty-five children – in this one room?"

"Yes."

"Golly gosh! I've never seen twenty-five children together anywhere, except on the telescreen. Wasn't it noisy?"

"Sometimes, but not when they were all reading or writing or listening to my story."

The boy glanced down at the watch swinging from his belt. Then he jumped up, letting the desk crash back to the floor. It raised puffs of dust.

"Hey, time's getting on. I'd better be going. They'll be worrying about me. Look, will you be here tomorrow afternoon?"

"Yes, I'll be here tomorrow afternoon."

With that promise in his ears, Terry was gone, feet banging through the dusty corridors, swing doors slamming after him. Charles caught a glimpse of the black head bobbing along the other side of the wall, then all was quiet again.

"A boy!" Charles told the silent, dusty room. "A real live boy who never once said I was a silly old fool for playing out a fantasy. It feels like a dream!" But his heart was lighter as he carefully locked the school doors and set off for home, the promise of tomorrow in his eyes.

For three days Terry came in the afternoons, banging through the old swing doors, shouting his greeting, dusty corridors echoing his voice. Together the old man and boy bridged the gap of years, poring over dusty browning books, rustling pages in the afternoon heat of the lovely summer days. Terry laughed at words that stayed still, watched with amusement as Charles chalked simple mathematics on the blackboard and wiping them off with the eraser as cleanly as the processor cleared the screen for another lesson. For three days Charles felt as if the clock had been turned back; he was a complete person again, doing what he had always loved best.

At the end of the third afternoon, Terry scuffed his feet and looked out of the window, hesitating.

"My telescreen's been fixed; I start lessons again tomorrow."

"That's all right, Terry." The lump in his throat threatened to choke him. He turned away, pretending that the mist in front of his eyes was the heat haze.

"I've – I've really enjoyed the lessons." Terry seemed afraid of the emotion he could feel from Charles, as if not sure how to handle it.

"Thank you. It's been good to teach again for a while."

"Will you still come here?"

"I expect so." Charles took a deep breath and turned back to look at the trusting, sad face. "I've been doing it for a long time. No one seems to care and it gives me something to do."

"It must be lonely, being old." And for a moment the sadness was almost too much for Terry to bear.

"It is." Charles forced a smile which didn't reach his eyes. "Thank you, Terry; you gave me back my past for a little while. Go on with you now. Your family will start worrying about you again. I'll be all right. I'll be here when the telescreen breaks down again."

"Sure." Terry got up, anxious not to delay the parting, seeming to want to be alone. "Bye, Charles." And for the last time Terry ran from the classroom, pounding the dusty corridors, letting the doors swing shut behind him.

It was a long time before Charles could bring himself to leave the empty room, still filled with Terry's vibrant energy and youth. Tomorrow would be emptier than ever before. At last he slowly locked the doors and windows and left with a heavy tread.

The next day Charles stood at the window, not even attempting to pretend he was there for any other reason than to grieve for the friendship he had found – and so quickly lost.

"I shouldn't have come," he told himself. "The dream's gone, everything's changed. I'll never be able to imagine it again."

Suddenly he thought he heard Terry calling and shook his head. He was dreaming; he had to be. Terry was at home, studying in front of the faceless soulless telescreen.

60

"Come on, Gran, he's in here! He said he'd be here." Terry burst through the door, radiating excitement. Behind him came an old lady, hair as white as his own, face wreathed in wrinkles and smiles.

"Charles, this is my Gran. She's lonely too."

A touching of hands, a mutual smile. Charles felt his depression slip away. Perhaps the long years wouldn't be so lonely after all…

This story is dedicated, with respect and admiration, to the memory of the great SF writer Isaac Asimov, who planted a seed many years ago with his story "The Fun They Had" published by F&SF. In the story children had a telescreen to give them their lessons and, having discovered 'real' books and schools, were sad to think of the fun those children had had and the lonely lives the modern children led. I took that theme and created my own version as a tribute to a great writer.

Poetry and Ice Cream (Rickey Rivers Jr.)

Pat was in the backyard, sitting on the ground, staring off into the distance. Sam left their home to meet him.

"What's up?" she called.

"Hey," he said, looking up.

Sam sat down beside him. "What you doing?"

"Writing"

The pen and pad were close, but far from reach.

"Writing without writing tools? That's a new one."

He smiled. "At the moment I'm thinking."

"Oh, the thinker thinks!"

Pat laughed. "Yeah, that's right."

"You know I never really got much into poetry. I never understood it."

"What's to understand? Poetry is life."

"You've said that before, but it doesn't make sense."

Pat thought about it. "Have I told you the story of my English teacher from high school?"

"No, I don't think so."

"Well, it's not too long, or eventful. First off this teacher was a stoic woman, no nonsense, not really mean but firm. I never saw her laugh. Still, you could tell she cared and wasn't just there to be there, you know?"

"Sure, a good teacher, do you remember her name?"

"Not at the moment…" He trailed off.

"So, that's it then?"

"Oh no, I'm sorry. Back in the day we had an assignment about the analysis of literature and how it reflects the world around us. I got a C and a bunch of red marks. The teacher wanted me to stay after class. She said she knew I could do better. I didn't believe that. Back then I didn't believe in myself much." He paused, chewed his lower lip. "A few weeks later I waited after class and gave my teacher a poem I had worked hard on. She smiled as if she knew something. Then she read the poem to herself."

Sam looked on. Pat's eyes were on the horizon, watery, further away than usual.

"Well," he went on, "I know how it sounds but I swear I saw a twinkle in her eyes. Magic, a little bit of light brought to her from a faraway place. She handed back the poem and simply said 'good work'. Her next class began soon so I had to leave. I didn't understand at the time, but I got older."

"…so what was the poem about?"

"Whatever it was, it affected her greatly."

"Obviously"

A gust of wind blew. It shuffled his notepad. Neither of them paid it attention. Sam gave him a stare. His mouth hung open. His eyes were not on her. His hands were together, one in the other.

"So what was it about?" she said.

"What?"

"The poem! Do you still have it?"

"No… possibly…I don't know."

Sam's nose crinkled as she pressed her lips against her teeth. "What was the point of that story?"

63

"I thought you wanted to understand poetry?"

"I do! I thought I did. I still don't understand." Sam shook her head.

Pat gave a smile and put a hand on hers. Her hand was cool on the warm grass. His hand was heavy and bones.

There was an ice cream truck jingle somewhere in the neighborhood.

"This is beautiful," he said. A bit of his hair blew in the breeze.

"Yeah, I guess," said Sam. Her gaze went from him to sunset and back again. As always, she had questions.

"I want to be with you forever," he started. "But I know that's impossible."

"…what brought that on?"

"Just a thought, I'm not so young."

She sighed. "Stop talking like that. I don't want to think about it."

Children could be heard. They were either chasing the ice cream truck or fighting each other over a cone.

Pat gave her a look, it pierced her, gave her a terrible feeling, like pulling wood from a wound. His eyes watered.

"What's wrong?" she asked, clutching his hand.

"Nothing, just thinking."

In due time the sun set completely. They let time outside linger for as long as it feasibly could. The ice cream truck was somewhere further away.

"We could chase it," said Sam.

"You could," said Pat.

"No, it wouldn't taste the same without you."

Elsewhere the children seemed content with ice cream. Pat's notepad was still open. The wind made the pages flutter from time to time. Soon the pages were still. And Sam was running.

The Hole (SJ Townend)

Surely all children are cared for? That's what parents and teachers do, right? Our table of eight agreed firmly on this over high tea whilst discussing the engraved words we had all seen: 'Hawthorn House for Cared for Children'. The text was chipped into the freshly mounted plaque by the double doors of the townhouse neighbouring our school. The Victorian building, vacant for a while, desperately needed doing up. I took a sip of my milky tea, bit the glacier cherry off from the top of my Chelsea bun and listened in to the gossip before Ms. Lonsdown escorted us to the changing rooms to get changed for lacrosse.

"Total amelioration," I'd overheard Mother saying whilst chin-wagging at pick-up amongst a gaggle of parents. They were all clucking over whether our school should purchase it as an additional boarding house or perhaps convert it into an additional sporting facility.

Us girls were used to it being empty, with its shut-eye sealed windows and its overgrown acre of lawn. For as long as any of us could remember, the scruffy meadow which backed onto our playground had been referred to as 'The Wilderness'. Its long grasses poked through our fence like prisoner's hands, totally out of bounds. But, at the start of term, year five noticed that it had been mown and that there were children on the other side of the barrier, too.

These children didn't look like us, though; similar in size and shape, yes, but there were no cord-trimmed blazers and matching berets, no knee-socks and polished leather penny loafers. Their teeth hung crooked, orthodontically-challenged if you like and many were unquestionably in dire need of a trip to the hairdressers.

These were poor children, not cared for children. These were children whose parents couldn't, wouldn't, or shouldn't be present in their lives. We waved at the Cared for Children through the chicken wire fence and some of them waved back. A girl in vintage sportswear exchanged a smile with me, told me she liked my pigtails despite her eyebrow suggesting otherwise. A younger boy passed a stick of gum to Beatrice but wouldn't tell us his name.

Headmistress called an additional assembly on Tuesday, pushing Classics back by twenty minutes. We sat cross-legged, linear on the hard wooden floor facing the stage whilst she informed us of the 'project' next door and instructed us that we weren't to 'interact'. She spoke of the boys and girls who were spending time in the four storey building as if they were rescued animals, waiting to be re-housed; paperback rejects, dustily sitting on a library shelf.

"What if they don't get re-homed?" Beatrice bravely asked, but her question hung, unanswered.

***

It was morning break when Tallulah first noticed the hole in the chicken wire fence. The sky high patchwork of metal hexagons which separated us—pupils at the most expensive all-girls middle school in the South—from them, the Cared for Children who came and went like leaves rolling in the wind, was broken.

During a class discussion in History (Ms. Harrow had nipped to reprographics), we decided how awful it was that these children had been snatched, taken from their families and imprisoned in the house and the garden abutting our playground. At three, or six if we had hockey, day-pupils at our school were free as birds to go home for prep and supper. Even our boarders were granted exeat each weekend if they weren't tied up with lacrosse or rifle practice. How awful it was that our teachers considered these Cared for Children akin to livestock. Would our staff mount a plaque on our chicken wire fence, facing inwards towards our playground, warning us not to poke our fingers through for fear they might get bitten?

We hatched a plan followed by a democratic vote all before Ms. Harrow returned and a unanimous decision was made.

***

A buddleia bush concealed the edge of the fence, where the hole had called out to us. It provided adequate cover over lunch break. Most of our year got involved. Even Lori Taylor-Smythe, lone-wolf, huddled down by the gap, taking a turn to poke and scrape and keep watch as we all industrially excavated the soil beneath the hole with sticks and sharp-edged stones.

I've still no idea who instigated the project but I was elected to go first. Being the smallest usually means I get picked last for games and left out a lot, an odd sock of sorts, but at that moment, everyone wanted to be my friend and to pat me on the back. By the time I'd scuffled through—lickety-split—my knees grazed but not bleeding, I'd clawed away more dirt so more girls could trail behind me in turn and in under a minute, half of the year had followed me through. We poured along fractured lines like ants at a picnic, into the forbidden land.

The Cared for Children were scattered around a single swing, unsupervised, waiting in turn, but on spotting us invading their space, they started to charge. With raised, single index fingers to our lips, we crept forwards, towards them.

"Shhh," Beatrice spoke. "We come in peace. Be quiet or we'll get caught."

Fifteen Cared for Children gathered around us and settled, curious, unsure. Ice was broken with a shared bag of mint humbugs Verity had smuggled from tuck duty as we chatted briefly and articulated our idea, as each of us picked stuck shards from our teeth. Both tribes fired closed answer questions at low volume until they offered us a tour.

We turned them down, not because we knew there would be no heated pool or equestrian centre, or because we were fearful of getting caught, but because our plan was better; magnificently so.

"There's no time," Emily said before pulling our conspicuous gathering closer to the bushes.

Tallulah then unfurled logistical suggestions to the Poor Children as our year stood with clasped hands and broad grins until they all nodded in merry agreement.

Lydia, or possibly Amelia-Jane, was the first to start stripping down I think, but my memory is most unreliable; full of conjugated Latin verbs, no space for anything else. I was far too excited to be taking details in. Everything happened so fast. Whoever it was, a sweater was peeled off, tossed, then an unknotted, striped necktie was flung into the exchange pool. Swiftly, the rest of us followed suit. Some girls traded entire uniforms, others, just a sock or a hat or a shoe.

Once the outfit swap was complete, we led them back through the hole in the fence and they followed us into Mathematics. Four cheeks to a seat, we crammed into the classroom; new friends were made, stories were spilled. A hysterical cacophony filled the air and Poor Ms. Kingswell, try as she did, could not quieten us down. Immediately twigging that there were faces she did not recognise, double numbers present, she marched out and down the polished corridor towards Headmistress's office, steaming as if she might boil over.

Headmistress and a man and a woman whom none of us recognised appeared in our classroom faster than a quarter horse and ushered the Cared for Children back out through the door, assuring Headmistress that our uniforms would be returned later that week, freshly laundered and pressed. I swear one of the adults, the chap, found it funny—

his lips curled up at the corners as he apologised profusely whilst reversing his way out.

Our entire year was frogmarched into the hall and became cross-legged again on the solid oak floor.

"Which of you is responsible for this outrageous calamity?" screeched Headmistress, rolling her 'R's, hurting our ears. The skin on her neck webbed, shrink-wrapping her ligaments, as her jaw jutted backwards and forwards. Out hurled her angry speech, each word slapping.

"There will be consequences!"

None of us spoke or dared to move. Consequences? We hadn't thought about the consequences. Aftermath unravelled as angular and jagged and as uncomfortable as the edges of the disentwined chicken wire fence had been.

"You will sit here until a name is put forwards. You will be disciplined."

Six teachers stood, fanned out, behind our livid headmistress, a peacock tail of reinforcement; all arms crossed, all eyes probing and all faces stern. Seconds turned into minutes but not one of us broke. Perhaps only one of us, tops, knew who was responsible anyway. And my memory is most unreliable.

The gallery clock above the stage read two minutes to three. I was starting to worry about Mother. I knew she would be sitting in her four-by-four in the car park waiting to shuttle me across to horse riding. She'd be spitting feathers. I glanced sideways at Tallulah who was picking at strips of

71

dead skin around her fingernails. Her father would be waiting too, his heels well and truly cooled.

The reality of the situation landed like a broken aeroplane; in a matter of minutes, parents were going to be involved.

Despite our apprehension, tenacious loyalty bound us tight. Friendship wove us together into an obstinate quilt of girls as secure as the undamaged parts of the fence and, as I discretely looked at Tallulah, then Emily, before glancing back at my year behind us, I just knew. We would move as one.

"We can all see that it's three," said Headmistress, aware of young eyes drawn to the clock. "If you think you are going anywhere however, you are most mistaken. Mr. Piper, Ms. Ashworth, let the parents know we're running over. Bring them forth if necessary."

She dusted imagined lint from her jacket and straightened her skirt. "This is your last chance, girls. Come clean now. Look at you all, dressed in other people's clothes, dirty clothes. I am disgusted by your behaviour."

She slammed the rubber tip of her walking cane three times hard. Floorboards shook.

"Who. Is. Responsible?"

I watched the two teachers scarper, witch's minions and then, with a bellyful of nerves and a smidge of hope, I slowly raised my hand. "It was me, Headmistress. I started it."

Almost in sync, Tallulah raised her hand too.

"And me, Miss. It was my idea too."

Headmistress's face had reddened to the colour of a finger chilli. I cornered my head with impish excitement, ever hopeful, I faced the girls behind me—

Every single hand, lifted.

Every.

Single.

One.

We spoke united.

Headmistress fell tongue-tied as mothers and fathers trickled in through the side door and huddled at the back of the hall.

"Hands down, girls," she cracked with clenched jaw and furrowed brow before softening her posture and tone to address her guests, her benefactors.

"Please come in, come in. Come and collect your dear daughters."

Headmistress lifted her stick-free palm up towards the ceiling, a sign we've all been trained to understand: rise. Obediently, we took to our feet and moved with method, like glass chess pieces, towards our respective parents.

"You may go home now, girls," she said, spitting out words like silent bullets through the forced smile on her chalk-white face, then off she scurried, stick in hand, through the curtains at the back of the stage, up the corkscrew staircase, up to her office.

***

Mother tried her best to withhold laughter when I told her what had happened, how the fence pulled us through, yet she also seemed concerned.

73

"Why weren't any of you being watched?" she asked, her French-tips tapping on her filigree necklace and, although I tried to persuade her not to, she insisted on phoning Headmistress to complain. We still made it on time for horse riding, if you were wondering. I cleared a two-foot jump.

The next day, break happened as normal. Even tuck opened up, which none of us had expected. As we cascaded out of Physics and into the playground, we noticed that the hole that had caused the mix up had been patched back up, lickety-split. It was never mentioned again.

We waved at the Cared for Children through the fence. They waved back and smiled as they waited in line for their swing.

Hush-a-bye, Baby (Rie Sheridan Rose)

"I'm sorry. The situation proved to be more complicated than we originally anticipated. We did discuss this possibility. I'm sorry it proved to be the case. There was nothing else we could do—"

Cora stared down at her hands, knotted tightly on the chenille spread. "It's all right," she answered, in her soft drawl. "God's will be done." She smiled tremulously at the doctor, but her eyes were dry.

"Well, if I can do anything, just let me know."

Cora's throat worked convulsively as she fought the impending tears. You didn't cry in front of strangers. Her mother had drummed that into her head. Her mother...

"I'll check in tomorrow," the doctor promised, patting her arm in consolation. "You get some rest."

After he left the room, Cora faced the wall and let the storm break. Disconsolate tears were counterpointed by ugly, racking sobs that tortured her throat and sutured abdomen. They had assured her the operation was standard procedure. They had intimated there should be no permanent repercussions. They had said the prognosis was good. They had made it seem mere routine to sign the consent form, "Just in case."

They had apologized when there were complications.

The problem had been irreparable. They had removed her entire uterus. It didn't help that the organ appeared to have been dysfunctional—what mattered was that she could never have children...

When she had married young, they had been cutting corners so closely that it seemed prudent to wait before having children. There would be time... and then Jerome's convertible slammed into a truck, killing him instantly. She never even got to say goodbye.

It had taken her four years to crawl out of that pit. She had begun to toy with the idea of having a baby alone. She had even made some inquiries— before they rushed her to the hospital for the emergency surgery and dashed her hopes again...

After the initial shock had died away and they shooed her out of the hospital like a good little girl, she drifted back to her empty apartment and her oh-so-proper career at the bank. Everyone was very solicitous and somehow that made it worse. She just couldn't take the kind looks and the whispers. The management was generous with their severance package and it gave her a little breathing space.

However, it didn't take long for the novelty of being a person of leisure to wear off. It gave her too much time to dwell on what she couldn't change. It was a spur-of-the-moment decision really. She was walking by the daycare center and saw the sign in the window.

They were only looking for a general support person, so her lack of child-care experience didn't worry them. Even the drastic pay cut was worth it, because it gave her a chance to connect with children. She would sit on the floor, listening to the toddlers with grave attention. The youngsters responded to her with an unconditional love that went a long way toward soothing the dull ache inside.

***

Two months after she started the job she first met Benny Chamberlain. It was love at first sight for Cora. When they met, Benny—a solemn-eyed three-year-old whose tousled blond curls tangled engagingly over his forehead—hunkered silently with his back pressed tightly into the corner.

"My name's Cora. What's your name?" she asked softly, kneeling before him.

Hope lit his eyes. "Can we pretend you're my mommy?"

Cora's heart contracted. "We can do that," she promised recklessly, holding out her arms.

The little boy melted into them. "My name's Benny," he whispered, his breath warm in her ear.

During the afternoon, Cora learned that Benny's mother had died six weeks earlier. His father, a corporate vice-president, didn't seem to have much time for Benny.

"Poor baby," Cora sighed, eyes misting. "He doesn't understand any of this, does he?"

After learning some of the details of Benny's home life, Cora spent every moment she could with Benny, the numbness inside slowly dissolving under the sunshine of his shy smile. In six months, she never saw his father, Landon Chamberlain, apart from his pulling up outside and honking the horn for Benny. It grated on Cora's nerves that the man never even left the car. He didn't deserve a fine boy like Benny.

Cora helped Benny into his coat one afternoon and the little boy gazed up at her with his soulful eyes and murmured, "Cora..."

"What, baby?"

"I wish it wasn't just pretend. I wish you were my real mommy."

Cora swept him into her arms, hugging him tight. "So do I, sweetheart, but you know I can't be. Your daddy loves you—"

"But he's always busy with Debbie. He don't have time for me."

Cora's blood boiled. Chamberlain not only neglected his son, but also spent all his time with a woman instead? How dare he!

"Hush-a-bye, baby," she soothed Benny. "Everything will be all right."

The more Cora thought about Chamberlain's treatment of Benny, the angrier she became. It would serve the man right if Benny simply disappeared one day...

Well, why not? She loved Benny and Benny loved her. They needed each other and Landon Chamberlain hardly knew his son existed. She could take Benny away. They could start their own little family. Look how many milk carton kids vanished, even in this cybernetted wonderland...

Cora sat down hard on the tile floor, still clinging to Benny. How could she even consider such a thing? Stealing the boy wouldn't make him hers. It would be worse than illegal. It would be

78

immoral. It would do to Chamberlain what had been done to her.

There was a loud honk outside and Cora set Benny down, ruffling his hair. She could at least do something about that!

"Let's go talk to your daddy," she winked, taking Benny's hand. "Maybe he'll take you for pizza... would you like that?"

Benny nodded with delight, eyes shining. Cora marched purposefully to the curb.

A man with Benny's beautiful eyes unfolded himself from the front seat of the waiting car, smiling wearily. "You must be Cora," he commented, extending his hand. "I'm Landon Chamberlain. Benny has told me all about you."

"Mr. Chamberlain—" Cora began, but an imperious wail cut her off.

"Hush-a-bye, baby," Chamberlain murmured, lifting an infant from the car. He jiggled her against one hip. "I'm sorry. I can't leave Debbie alone in the car and getting her trussed into and out of the car seat is more than I can take just to run inside for Benny. I know he's had to grow up too fast lately, but my wife died right after the baby was born. It's been rather hectic, juggling the kids and work..."

Cora's preconceptions shattered like glass when she noted the shadows under Chamberlain's eyes and the gentle caress he gave Benny. This was not some unfeeling corporate playboy. This was a loving father struggling with far more than anyone should have to handle alone...

With a proud, paternal grin, Chamberlain bent to listen to Benny's urgent whisper as the boy tugged on his sleeve. "Pizza? Sounds great, sport. Would you care to join us?" Landon asked Cora, his eyes showing he was genuinely interested.

Debbie started to whimper and Cora held out her arms instinctively. "May I?"

Chamberlain handed her the baby with a grateful sigh and Cora nestled Debbie against her shoulder, murmuring, "Hush-a-bye, baby…"

"You're a natural," Chamberlain observed.

"Mr. Chamberlain—"

"Landon—after all, we're about to break pizza together."

"Landon," she amended shyly. "Would you be interested in a little free baby-sitting? I bet you don't get out much by yourself these days…"

"I accept—on one condition. You let me take you out to dinner one night. Without Benny. You can consider it payment if you like."

"That would be lovely," she smiled and—for the first time in a long time—she felt as if there was a little something to look forward to in her life.

Every Cloud (SJ Townend)

Each paper cut I have ever received has brought on an April shower, irrespective of the season. Each grazed knee has brought forward a monsoon.

For a time, in my teens, I would experiment with the sharp end of the compass from my trigonometry kit. When I'd mastered some control over my power, I used it to my advantage. I'd etch crossed eyes, a wobbly grin with a tongue poking from it onto the back of my hand—Nirvana—and wait for the rain to come.

I started to use my ability to bring on poor weather every Wednesday at three after enduring double maths. I enjoyed mathematics, I didn't enjoy the hockey which followed. I would sit at the back of the classroom, balancing my text book upright on my desk to create an opaque windscreen with which I shielded myself, I drove the stainless steel needle back and forth through my skin; just enough to make the red flow. Then the rain would start, pitter-patter and hockey would get called off. Another Wednesday afternoon would be spent in the library instead of out on the cold pitch. I would huddle up with a book and pretend to read whilst listening to the syncopated drumming of water on the roof, occasionally dabbing the back of my hand with blue tissue, until home time came.

Eventually a teacher noticed what I was doing eventually and referred me to counselling. I didn't bother explaining to the biscuit-proffering serious lady with the half-moon glasses how much I hated sport, or how much I despised having to change into my gym kit in front of the other girls—all curves, all hair—as I stood, ashamed, flat and smooth. I didn't bother mentioning that I controlled the weather with my bodily fluids either, as I presumed everyone did this. The skin on the back of my hand was growing tired of it all anyway and Ms. Clark took away my trigonometry set.

***

My father liked a ladder and a power tool. I remember vividly when I was nine when he called my name twice. I had been sitting in the garden. It'd been hot so my dolls were drinking 'iced lemon tea' concocted with leaves from Mum's begonias and crud from the compost heap. The first time my father had called politely, but I ignored him, as was standard practice in our house—I had been too engaged in my game for whatever beetle or flower he wished to show me. The second time he'd yelled out my name, it had come from somewhere guttural. He'd called with the black notes I had never heard him sing with before. One way t6o gain my attention, I had run up the grey path to the large bush and the yellow legs of his tallest ladder.

"What is it, Dad? Found another nest?"

"Get your mother," he'd replied. I saw the hedge-trimmer several metres away on the ground, its toothed saw buzzing hungrily. My father was at the top of the ladder, not holding it.

"Now!" he shouted and it was then I saw the blood. This wasn't trigonometry blood, the type

82

which could be caught and spread on blue tissue, folded and pressed into teenage Rorschach ink blot tests. This blood of my father was adult-sized blood. I saw blood that could be collected in demijohns and vases. This blood had been pumping out, erupting in bursts into the air, splattering onto leaves and his shirt. It came in flurries, keeping time with my heartbeat and with each squeeze of his. It made a mess of his top and the buddleia.

"She's in the kitchen," I said as my father vomited into the space between us. I had run toward where my mother would be, hearing the spray of falling carrot and stomach lining hailing down onto the path behind me; I, Napalm Girl all flailing limbs, him, hand and throat, explosive. It sounded like the start of a storm but smelled of yesterday's roast and beer. I discovered my mother chopping offal and brought her out to Dad. She helped him down from the ladder, steadied him into the car, taking on board most of his weight despite being half his size. His face had become as pallid as the cloud that had drawn over the sun and as ghostly as the bath towel Mother had yanked from the washing line to wrap around his hand and stump. The white towel had become deep red by the time we arrived at the hospital.

"Carry this, keep it steady. Don't look inside," Mum had said, her hands shaking as she'd passed me something gift-sized and wrapped in a clean tea towel. I held the tip of his finger in that Tupperware box for three miles, never once looking at it, but knowing every time my father screamed in pain that it was there, dying, cell by cell. He had screamed a lot but he never shed a tear.

"Your father has lost several pints of blood," said the surgeon who had come to speak to us as my father lay heavily medicated in a faraway room. "But he should make a full recovery." I had wanted to ask how they knew. How did they know how much blood had drained and spurted out from him—had they weighed him? It? How did they top him back up? I had imagined three glass jugs full to the lip with his equivalent loss sat on the windowsill of the hospital ward, waiting to be tipped back down his stump before they could reattach the nail nubbin. His nail never grew back,and he can't feel anything in his index finger, but he's still alive. He had been very lucky. People die from lesser injuries, so the surgeon had told us.

Despite all his blood loss, it hadn't rained at all that day. So that is how I knew I was different to my father.

***

My mother bled from her gums nearly every time she brushed her teeth. My father said that a grey cloud followed her around wherever she went, but her gum disease never made it rain. She was not a wet person, in fact, as she grew older, she became drier. For a while I kept a chart of the times I'd seen her spit red with white when we had groomed ourselves for the day ahead together in the bathroom, before my breasts came, before I was made to use the downstairs bathroom alone for my ablutions. There seemed to be no significant overlap between her bleeding from her mouth and the weather, so I knew that I was different to my mother. But I noticed that each of the three times she lost an adult tooth, someone our family knew died.

A great uncle who we spent summer with several years ago but whose face I could not recall was first, then an elderly lady with a face like a brain coral who smelled sulphurous and sickly, like science experiments. She visited every few weeks, coercing my mother into buying toiletries from a small catalogue. They stank of chemicals. She would stand on our doorstep and talk at my mother about how her husband, who none of us had ever met, was having problems with his prostrate. I'd heard her sales pitch so many times that I'd looked the word up in the library dictionary whilst avoiding hockey on a wet Wednesday. It made no sense to me why a man would spend so long lying face down when there was so much to see in the world. Perhaps he was afraid of the rain.

It was a relief when she passed, the doorstep catalogue lady, although no-one said so out loud. None of us liked the astringent fragrances in the shower gels that had accumulated in the bathroom. We'd all said that out loud and, even at the age of ten, I could read between the lines.

***

I bought my first pair of heels when I was thirteen. Of course, they made me bleed. I used money I'd saved from washing cars at the place where my father worked. I walked two miles into town in the bastard footwear, with no socks on, to try and break them in. The imitation leather won that battle. By the time I'd reached Ourprice—to rummage through the cassette bargain bin—my heels were in agony. I tried to wedge some tissues down the back of my shoes to sop up some of the blood, but it had stung so much I took them off, slung them into my bag and walked through town barefoot. A murder scene trail of blood played out behind me as I marched to the bus stop.

Of course, the heavens opened as soon as my heel skin had broken. As soon as the first red drop had trickled down my heel, along the ridge of the shoe and made its way to the front of my foot where I had noticed it, the bad weather had started. I got drenched waiting for the bus. The rain came down sideways, as did my eyeliner.

***

The first time I bled from my vagina, lightning and thunder joined the party. It had started in the night. I remember waking damp and warm in my bed which smelled of copper pennies. I'd switched on my bedside lamp and looked down between my legs, expecting a river of sweat to be flowing out from the space between my thighs, as this is what my dream had suggested. But it was not sweat, it was blood. Mother had prepared me for this day by showing me a leaflet that came with a pack of pads resembling small mattresses. She'd put the pads in my underwear drawer and the pamphlet in the bin. School had told us that enough blood to fill an egg cup would come out each month along with an unused egg. I could see no egg as I pawed through the mess on my sheets, using tissues to try and clean it up, although—the gloop did have the texture of clotted yolk. Mother heard the thunder that night and she came into my room.

"Get the pads," she said. "Go and wash yourself. I'll put on new sheets." We never spoke about that night again.

It felt most unnatural, wearing a pad, like having a swim noodle between one's legs, like straddling a hot dog bun. I couldn't get back to sleep, even with fresh sheets so instead of trying, I sat on my windowsill in the dark, watching the rain pour down outside until I saw enough water collect on the ground to weigh down my eye lids.

It rained for five days straight and then ended abruptly, as the eleventh pad in the pack remained white.

***

As I grew older, my monthlies became heavier and, with them, the weather grew worse. In my mid-twenties, I remember a camping trip which had to be abandoned as I came on in the night. I had an idea it was coming—I could see grey clouds gathering in the late afternoon sky and my stomach had been cramping, dealing with some internalised thunder. I retired early, leaving the others to toasted marshmallows and beer from plastic cups as I curled up in my sleeping bag. It had been the middle of summer, but I woke in the night to find I had leaked from the 'heavy flow' pad I'd stuck in my knickers. My torch beam revealed clots of congealed red stuck to the lining of my sleeping bag as the tent started to leak. I screwed the sleeping bag up into a bin bag and wiped myself down with an old t-shirt minutes before my friend woke. The water poured in on us through a slit in the canvas, and the wind picked up outside. Drops of rain the size of golf balls pounded on the taut canvas making warzone sounds as blood gushed from me, soaking through pad after pad; I was leaking from the inside out and also from the outside in. We decided to pack down and abandon ship. It must have been three in the morning. After an hour bent over, yanking out pegs in horizontal rain, we managed to fold everything up sloppily into the boot of our car. We drove all the way back home in the midst of the night and I spent the rest of the week in bed with a cold. It rained until my period finished.

***

I found it hard to tell people about my situation, my power and, with time, I learnt that people didn't really want to know. A boyfriend had ended things with me shortly after I'd explained to him that I couldn't go boating at the weekend—it was my time of the month and bad things might happen at sea. Or out on the lake.

"When I bleed, it rains," I'd said to him.

"It's not me, it's you," he'd replied.

***

Many years later, in my mid-thirties, I met a man who understood me. I told him over coffee, after we'd decided to move in together. I thought it best he know, before contracts were signed, dates set —he would find out otherwise, eventually. Some people can handle the rain and always carry an umbrella, others, not so much.

"So, sometimes when I bleed, the weather changes. For the worse," I'd said as he'd bit into his lemon drizzle cake. His eyes always shone kindness, like the sun. This was one of the reasons why I loved him.

"I understand," he said. "My mother used to get that too." He kissed me and told me that when it rained, he'd be there to make a rainbow. Then he offered me a piece of his cake.

We moved in together and things were perfect for a while. He taught me how to go out in the rain, how to embrace the bad weather. We bought puddle suits and wellington boots and made light of it all and he showed me how to see beauty in the floods that my bleeding body seemed to bring.

One day, things became torrential outside. I was curled up on the sofa—hot water bottle on my belly, mug of hot chocolate in my hand. It was in this moment that he asked me to marry him. It was in this moment that I said yes. Then he pressed his forefinger gently to my philtrum and told me there was something he needed to tell *me* first, before I agreed. There was something I needed to know about *him*.

"Go ahead," I said. "Nothing you can tell me will make me love you any less." He smiled and squeezed my hand.

"When I fall in love, I bleed," he said, his smile falling away, joining a puddle with my fresh tears.

When he fell in love, he bled.

I didn't understand at first, but as time went on, I grew to learn that he was a fan of trigonometry too and his body had the scars to prove it. He told me he had been in love before and had bled throughout that relationship. He told me he knew he was in love with me the moment after our first kiss—he had rushed home to let a little of his blood out. He pointed at the scars just below his ankle. He showed me more evidence on the soles of his feet. He said bleeding from his feet meant no-one would ever need to know.

Except for me.

I told him his secret was safe. I understood. And so we carried on and when I bled, it rained and he loved me and when he loved me, his feet wept tears of red.

***

A year into our relationship I became pregnant and the sun put his hat on for six months straight. People spoke of global warming, but I knew there was more to it than this.

My periods ceased—which was expected—and we shopped for small things. My partner got through a lot of socks.

One day, after six months of pure sunshine, I was driving home from work when I felt a sensation, a dampness and a warmth in my groin that had been so familiar, so often and so regular so many moons ago. I pulled over into a lay-by, undid my seatbelt and wrapped an arm around my swollen belly. I put my hands between the top of my thighs and felt for something. I pulled my fingers up and out and held them up in the air in front of me, I knew straightaway a storm was brewing. My fingers were red, dripping with blood.

I opened the door, got out of the car and looked down at the driver's seat where a lagoon had collected. The clouds drifted in front of the sun before my eyes, carrying the grey weight of the world's water in them. I reached for my phone and called my partner as the first drop of rain landed on my cheek.

The coldness of it all.

More blood came out of my body, down my legs and with the blood came pain. With the pain came a crack and a fork of lightning putting its angry fingers in fields which draped over the horizon. A deluge came and stayed.

He found me in the lay-by and took me to the hospital where our baby gave up on us. A parent who brought rain and another with chopping board feet—I don't blame the poor soul for checking out. That day the rain fell more heavily than I had ever seen and continued to fall heavily for a month. We drove home from the hospital and cried more tears as the sky cried with and on us.

A one hundred foot tsunami on the other side of the planet wiped out quarter of a million people at some point in the days that held our grief. A tidal wave taller than a blue whale, a wall of water higher than a ten story building, carrying more energy than one and a half thousand H-bombs rose up from the depths of the Indian Ocean and pushed forward, onto the land. I felt the pain of every single person I killed as I bled. I brought down a drop of rain for each of those who died.

When my bleeding ended, the sunshine never returned and my partner stopped dragging blades through his feet.

Lured To Kill (Olivia Arieti)

Timothy had always been wacky but not insane although most people were convinced of the opposite. His clumsiness and simpleton attitude increased the beliefs. After his parents' death and sisters' marriages, he went on living alone in the family home. He often dropped in the town's pub where, dressed in outdated attire, he would sit draining one beer after the other and look gloomily out of the window as though expecting someone. Nobody had ever been successful in starting a conversation with him. Now and then he sighed as if in pain or smiled slightly as though relishing a pleasant memory. Only when a pretty girl came in he would raise his eyes and cast a wistful glance at her. He had always hoped to meet his sweetheart, but no lass in the whole town would have ever dreamt of being seen around with him.

Long walks in the countryside were his favourite pastime although the landscape wasn't too inviting; lanes flanked by uncouth vegetation and barren trees. Most of the fields were abandoned and left to the scuffling of wild animals. The locals believed that the dead, too, when tired of lying in their graves, trod the solitary paths just to stretch their skeleton limbs.

In particular, the spirits of those who had been murdered and there were quite a few, would venture there, anxious to encounter their assassin and sooner or later take revenge.

It was on a winter afternoon when the sun died and left its salmon streaks to attenuate the upcoming darkness that Rachael crossed his path. She was wrapped in a hooded white coat and almost floated towards him.

"I've seen you more than once coming down this way, Sir."

Timothy gazed at her, "I'm afraid I don't know you, Miss," he muttered.

"Of course you don't, but I know you, Timothy... Such a handsome guy doesn't go unnoticed."

Unaccustomed to flattery, the young man blushed. He, in turn, was struck by the girl's beauty, blond curls framed her face brightened by sky blue eyes. She was thin and lean, had an evanescent aspect and seemed to have come out of the mist that suddenly had fallen upon them.

"I'm Rachel. Mind if we walk together?"

Without waiting for a reply, she took his arm; the warmth of her touch reached all his senses and he would have gone on walking forever.

"Where do you live?"

"Not too far from here."

While the guy was trying to figure out the place, as there were no houses in the nearby surroundings, Rachael whispered, "I like you, hon."

Timothy was totally confused, but relished every step he took by the charming stranger's side.

The girl stopped abruptly, let go of his hand and said, "I have to leave now, but we'll meet again, I look forward to it."

She vanished into the mist that had grown thicker as though a silent accomplice of the young lady's tricks.

Once at home, Timothy lit the fire, took out some wine and started drinking; one glass followed the other and before the bottle was empty and he was snoring in the armchair.

The wine made his reminiscences vague and conferred a halo of uncertainty to the previous day's encounter. Yet, the only thought of Rachael made him shiver with an unknown pleasure... He had to find out if she was for real and who she was.

***

The following morning, he took a drive to the outskirts of town. An old mansion near the graveyard caught his attention. Although the place looked abandoned and in such a bad state of deterioration that it possibly couldn't be inhabited, he pulled over.

The door was ajar and Timothy went in. After passing through a long corridor, he entered a huge living room. Cobwebs hung from the ceiling, layers of dust on the furniture and the candles of the silver candelabras were burnt out, the wax stiffened on the table; ashes only were in the fireplace that surely hadn't been used for ages. A tattered blanket and pillow with an embroidered case were on the sofa as though somebody had been sleeping there; on the wall was Rachael's portrait. She appeared a bit younger, but the intriguing eyes and languid smile were hers. Was that her home? It appeared more like the house of ghosts.

The dampness made him cough. He left hastily and went down to the pub.

After draining his second beer, he asked the barman, "Do you know anything about a girl named, Rachel? She lives somewhere in the countryside around here."

The guy stared at him, more surprised by the fact that he was finally talking to him than by the question.

"Why do you want to know?" he asked.

"Well, I just happened to meet her."

The reply would have startled him if he didn't know whom it came from.

The barman smiled weakly and said he'd heard of her but it was a very long time ago.

When he told his buddies of Timothy's question they laughed loudly, then silenced. The girl's story was too full of horror and pity, a dark secret that kept haunting the whole town.

***

Timothy's heart was throbbing as he walked down the lane early that evening and it throbbed even more when he saw Rachel heading towards him.

"I was waiting for you," she muttered, "I want to take you to my house," and led him to the same place he had visited in the morning.

Magically, it looked different. A bright fire was blazing in the fireplace, all candles were flickering and the dust and cobwebs had been swept away. The room was warm and the atmosphere most amiable. The house had acquired its past splendour.

Something strange was going on, but Timothy was too charmed by his hostess to care.

She offered him a drink, cuddled by his side and whispered, "I like you so much that I'd let you come upstairs with me if..." and there she paused and sighed deeply.

The young man was on fire; he took her hand and kissed it, already sensing the pleasure of feeling her body under his in the intimacy of her bed... It was the first time a girl had made advances towards him.

"What is it, Rachel?"

"My husband, he's mad, depraved and terribly jealous. He's beaten me more than once. I tried to run away but he always found me. The last time he swore he'd never let me go,"

"What a monster!" Timothy was horrified.

"There's only one way to have me, love," she said, determined, "you must kill him."

"Kill him?"

"Yes, sweetie, then I'll be free and totally yours... forever," she uttered alluringly and pressed her burning lips on his as if to seal the macabre deal.

Timothy would have done anything for her, even if it meant going straight to hell. Besides, he had a honourable reason to commit such a deed and felt like a valiant knight who had to rescue his maiden from a terrifying dragon.

He would fetch the guy and stab him with the knife Rachel had just given him then, triumphant, he'd return to his lover.

"Wilfred will come tonight, I'm sure of that."

"Does he live here?"

"No, we parted long ago, but he still checks on me. Now I'll go to my room and wait for you. When you've done, come up."

Timothy was perplexed. He didn't expect the fellow's arrival and the weapon in his hand looked frightening... The fire had fuelled his senses till then suddenly left him and he felt cold and uneasy. He had never killed a man.

Before he could reconsider the matter, Wilfred staggered into the room.

"Where are you, bitch?" he cried. "You won't get away with it this time. "

The voice was raucous, the face decrepit and the hair white. How could such a wretch be Rachel's husband? Surely he was in his nineties...

Whatever, he looked mean and scary; his appearance was so unreal that Timothy wondered if he came from the other world. There was no time for considerations, though, and when the man headed towards the staircase, he plunged the blade into his back.

An inhuman cried followed and the guy fell to the floor.

At once, Rachel ran down, clad only in a torn grey robe which partly made visible her lovely silhouette.

"At last he's dead!" she cried. "You don't know how long I've been waiting for this moment."

98

She took his hand and pressed it on her heart. Her skin was softer and whiter than a swan's plumage. Then, almost like a fairy or any other ethereal lissom being, she ran back upstairs followed by her lover, now more intrigued by her sensuality than upset by his crime.

The room was dark, the brocade curtains shutting out every glimpse of light and a purple bedcover conferred a macabre aspect to the four-poster bed. The image of a hearse flashed before him.

He was about to hold her in his arms when she stepped back and said, "You have to do one more thing for me, love. I'll never find peace till Hilda is alive. She wanted Wilfred all for herself and even more depraved than him, the slag took part in his most vicious and wicked deeds."

Timothy was taken aback; the horror of killing again was tremendous but also the thought of the humiliations and cruelties poor Rachel had to undergo was unbearable.

Tears began falling down her cheeks and, as she sobbed, her breasts shook softly; compassion and desire strangely melded, Timothy's wish to soothe her pain had turned into a morbid craving to caress her quivering body.

Her imploring glance made him promise he would take care of Hilda too.

***

The given address led him to a nearby town; the cottage looked as decayed as Rachel's house when

99

he first entered it. Timothy pushed the door open and, much to his surprise, instead of a gaudy lady oozing vice and sensuality from every pore, he found an old lady snoring heavily in a rocking chair. Her face was so covered with wrinkles that it was difficult to discern the lips. The semi-open eyes seemed to sneer, "So she has sent you, huh?"

Wilfred's picture stood on a chest of drawers, a shady but handsome young man, quite different from the one he'd murdered.

How could Rachel be scared of those two wrecks? Somehow, stabbing her was harder because of the glare, because of the many doubts overwhelming him... Was she really Hilda?

He had to keep his promise, no matter what.

The way back was long, this time horror was stronger than desire and the number of doubts increased at every step. Who was Rachel? True, he had madly fallen for her, but her whole being was so veiled in mystery that he felt disconcerted... A gelid premonition seized him.

When he approached her house, he noticed that it had reassumed its abandoned look, the door once again ajar, cobwebs and dust all around, the candles consumed and no dying embers in the fireplace, only sooty ashes remained. The same blanket and pillow were on the sofa, this time stained with blood... What was going on there?

"Rachel, where are you?" he shouted and ran upstairs.

The bedroom was empty, the torn robe on the floor resembled a shroud.

He rushed back down and stopped before Rachael's portrait. Her lips were curled in an ambiguous grimace... Was she smiling at him or sneering at his stupidity?

Somehow his steps led him to the graveyard; the twilight shades and silence were frightening and hollow presences seemed to hover above him... He shuddered when he saw his beloved's picture on a tarnished gravestone. The girl had died seventy years ago, it read, 'brutally murdered by evil hands.'

Full of rage and despair, Timothy cursed and swore, then he knelt down and burst into tears, the only thing he could do.

It Is Election Time ... (Shashi Kadapa)

It was election time in Dharwad, a town in South India with the two national parties, the BJees and the EmptyGong, in the fray. Candidates searched for election issues to grill their opponents and show that they could handle it better. A drunken dog became the issue with hilarious chaos.

04. 30 hrs Dharwad

Basya, an occasional seasonal worker and frequent drunkard, received his wages. E hurried to the arrack- country liquor shop of Jakati the bootlegger where he bought a pot of brew. He squatted outside he lit a beedi and started swigging. The work had worn him out and he fell asleep, very uncharacteristically leaving the pot half-full.

A stray gray mongrel came sniffing and lapped up the hooch. The raw spirit hit quickly, it staggered on splayed legs to the village square and toppled over at the intersection of four roads. The intersection had three religious places, religion majority H, religion minority M, religion minority C, and a police station all facing each other.

05. 00 hrs Dharwad

Religious leaders M and C were bitter enemies of H leader, not out of devotion to their faith, but out of jealousy that he got more donations while they got measly amounts from their tight-fisted backsliding flock.

102

They waited for elections as the candidates would seek their blessings. They looked for some incident so that they could settle the issue and make money. The candidates were only interested in getting votes of followers of all religions.

05.00 hrs Dharwad

Irya was a petty thief, anything that could be rolled, picked, dragged, pushed, shoved was pilfered. Thoughtlessly, he stole a large concrete pipe and rolled it to Pathan, the fence with a 24x7 service.

Pathan was angry and shouted "Le Irya, who will buy this pipe? Take it away." A frustrated Irya cursed and rolled it to the village centre and dumped it near the comatose dog. He kicked a broken pot which made it clatter near the drunk dog.

06.00hrs am Dharwad

A BJees campaigner came awake at the racket. He saw the comatose dog and Irya kicking something. Immediately, he started shouting, "Murder, the EmptyGong party has killed."

Others started shouting, "EmptyGong murderers."

They picked up EmptyGong election banners and flung them near the dog. His candidate Brahmagouda had distributed pots of hooch to the canvassers who were sleeping it off. Liquor and cash were the main inducements for canvassers and the electorate, who switched sides when the opposite party gave more.

Brahmagouda woke in a foul mood from an alcohol fumed sleep and cursed the disturbance.

"Le Shyama, what is happening?"

Shyma, his assistant, came back panting, "Goudare ... killed."

"Who got killed?"

"A dog!"

"So? They bark the whole night."

"Goudare, the BJees killed a dog, they flung our banners on it and blame us."

"What! How dare they?"

They rushed out and threw BJees banners near the dog. Brahmagouda started shouting. "Ho, citizens, look at these heartless BJees dogs who killed a dog! Will you vote for them? Vote for me, EmptyGong will stop these killers."

A campaign jeep rolled up with Veeranna Gouda the BJees candidate on board. He looked perplexed at the scene, at the sleeping dog with banners of both parties. The matter was explained. He was a wily agile fellow and shinnied to the roof of a shop.

"Wake up, citizens! Are your women and children safe from these EmptyGong killers? Today they killed a dog, tomorrow it will be your children, wife, mother, your sisters. Down with EmptyGong!"

His ardent supporters clambered up and stood beside him, raising raucous slogans. The EmptyGong members surrounded the shop, gesticulating and shouting. The shop owner watched, petrified with fear for his shop.

The thatched roof was old, ramshackle and leaked from every impossible hole. It caved in, bringing down the walls and everything. Veeranna cracked his head on a wooden shelf and a small trickle of blood oozed, staining his shirt.

Ramya, his assistant, spat out some beetle leaf and smeared the red colour juice on his master's head and clothes.

Veeranna staggered from the ruins "See, people! These EmptyGong tried to assassinate me. I will martyr myself and serve you till my last drop of blood."

"Down with EmptyGongs. Killers," his followers chorused.

The parties rushed in flinging bottles, hurling chairs, tearing banners and beating each other. The anonymity of the crowd gave them a chance to settle personal scores.

A bottle hit Brahmagouda and he bled. Someone took a photo of the contestants, the dog and the ruined shop. They were posted on Twitter, Facebook and trolls forwarded the images.

The religious leaders waited to see how they could profit from this development. The police watched, not daring to intervene and earn the wrath of either side.

0800 hrs Delhi

PR officers of EmptyGong and BJees were replying to emails and social media posts and were stunned when the images came up. They hurried to call their respective leaders about an apparent opportunity for the election cause.

Central HQ EmptyGong leader RBaba announced, "I had reared it from a puppy. We will give the dog a grand funeral, as per its religion and sanction Rupees 10 lakh for the martyr killed by the BJees."

The BJees leaders announced, "We announce Rs 5 lakhs to the next of kin of the rape victim of EmptyGong atrocities."

All English and regional news channel flashed the breaking news and asked viewers to call in.

A fight by TV panellists started about the religion of the dog. Religion H cremated, M buried with a kaftan- shroud, C buried in a wooden box.

"Breaking news! The ruling party and the opposition members have approached the Supreme Court to decide on the religion of the dog."

1000 hrs Delhi - The Supreme Court

The honourable Justice of the Supreme Court was busy. His solitude was broken by a horde of lawyers who prayed for an urgent hearing.

Government Lawyer RK: "Your honour, today a dog was killed... We pray that you decide the religion of the dog for appropriate funeral arrangements."

The learned Justice listened to the petitioners with increasing anger and interrupted them.

"Are you joking? The Bench has many matters of great importance and you want us to rule on this? Step down if you cannot govern. Get out before I file contempt of court charges on you for this frivolous suit. Quiet or I will issue a non-bailable arrest warrant."

The media lapped up this news with gusto. It was not every day that they saw pompous lawyers humiliated.

10.15 hrs Dharwad
The district collector arrived. He did not understand what was going on and neither did any officer.

People rushed around trying to find a dog that could be palmed off as the kin and earn them the next of kin' bounty. Strays were enticed with rotis, rice, samosa, mirchis.

Someone said that the dead dog was grey. Solution - 'get their wards painted grey.'

***

Noorbhai did automobile body work. A sign said, "Daenting, payenting, all models, any colur, blak, grean, wite, sprae payented."

He was surprised at the horde and the dogs. Perplexed, he sauntered over to them.

"Paint my dog," shouted the horde.

"Eh, what?"

He considered himself to be a master payenter and felt that such work was an insult to his profession.

"I will give 100 rupees, here, take 200, here take 1000."

Soon the horde had money and a dog.

Nahida, his massive wife, looked at the scene and shouted. "Queue here with 2000 rupees. What colour do you want?"

107

"Grey."

Nahida was very efficient and an opportunity recogniser. She gathered the fees and gesticulated menacingly at her husband, "Oye, come on, get to work."

The reluctant Noorbhai was henpecked but he cursed and started spraying. The dogs squirmed, howled, growled, barked, snapped, bit. Soon the lot was ready.

The horde confronted the district collector with their painted dogs demanding immediate payment of 5 lakhs. The collector did not know what to do. Frantically he called the Chief Minister, who asked him to wait.

10.20 hrs Dharwad

The funeral expense of 10 lakh had inflamed the masses and the three religious leaders. The leaders began shouting.

"In our holy books, the dog is a companion of our God. We have the divine right of funeral."

"What divine right? I saw it first."

Fiery exchanges continued with bluster, bravado, gasconaded, grandiloquence and what not.

***

Regional TV and national TV operators had descended on the sleepy and 'woke' town. They trained their cameras on the gathering.

Jakati the bootlegger was irrigating the masses with his watered hooch.

Vendors had set up stalls and were shouting, "Hot tea, sweets, bhajiys, mirchi, samosa, vadapav, cold drinks, soda, sugarcane juice, sweets…"

Clothes vendors screamed, 'Redy made, bermoda shorts, pantlonpyants, banians, underwar, topis, half pyants, sarees, blouses, bras, penties, parkars, chaddis, pyjams buy one get one free."

A footwear seller shouted, "Buy one shoe and get the other free."

A few enterprising vendors set up rides of merry-go-rounds while jugglers and magicians tricked. Ashraf Bhai had set up a mobile gambling van and was taking bets on who would win the funeral rites. Musicians were singing off-key item numbers. Drama companies enacted ribald scenes. It looked like a village fair.

The police did not know whether to guard the dog, keep away the warring religious leaders or control the festivities. One wrong move and the press would create viral movies of the atrocities, religious leaders would claim persecution and activists would claim violation of human rights.

The District Collector held his head in his hands, knowing it would roll. Police Inspector Patil tried to force the crowd back. Any mishandling would mean demotion and posting to a 'non-remunerative' place.

The contestants set up loudspeakers on their jeeps and extorted the crowd to vote for them.

A funeral pyre was readied, graves were excavated and a wooden crate was prepared with holy water and flowers. The din and noise was enough to wake the dead while the living feared for their lives.

12.00 hrs Dharwad

The afternoon sun had hit the crowd. It was hours since they had gathered and were impatient. The candidates increased the volume and screamed until their voices broke.

The painted dog owners were shouting, the paint was running and their wards were snapping.

The police were tense and expected the crowds to riot. The religious leaders had increased the decibels of their prayers.

***

No one noticed the dog as it jerked awake. It urinated on the concrete pipe and walked.

Religious leader H was the first to see and screamed, "Miracle, miracle! My prayers brought to life the dead dog! My God and my prayers are great."

Minority M and minority C leaders saw the dog walking.

"My one and true Lord the merciful, you answered my prayers! You brought the dead to life."

"Great merciful father in heaven. You have shown your mercy. I will make the cur confess."

Within seconds, the prayer for funeral turned to a prayer of thanks for giving life to the dead.

The police inspector shouted, "Catch the dog for evidence."

The wily slippery dog quickly vanished leaving the crowd cheated.

***

Basya stirred from his stupor to see the crowd. He glanced at the hooch pot. Empty! Incensed, he picked It u p and flung it, hitting an activist of a party.

"Murder, murder!"

There was chaos, stones and sticks were flung and fights broke out, the police rushed. TV cameras zoomed on the candidates and religious leaders as they fought.

A normal election day.

The Relic Thief (Chris Marchant)

They carefully adjust the glass case on the pedestal.

"OK, that looks perfect, let's put the barriers up next."

"Just putting the relic in here first." The priest carefully puts the finger bone on its satin cushion in the glass case. The assistant places the barriers around the pedestal. Suddenly there's a clattering noise coming from the robing room of the church. The two priests spin around and rush over to find out what's happened.

The thief comes out from under the bench, goes up to the pedestal and quickly grabs the bone. He glances around quickly, then heads towards the stairs with his prize. The priests return just as he disappears into the shadows.

"That was quite funny, that ginger cat trying to steal the stoles."

"It looked like a bit of a love affair."

"Well, we chased him off."

"The relic, it's gone!"

"What? How? The only entrances are through the robing room, or the locked main door and we were in the robing room."

"The thief must still be in here then."

"Right, I'll go upstairs, you check down here."

They separate and head off to find the thief. A ginger face peers round the edge of a door and a rather rotund ginger cat creeps towards the benches, dragging a green stole behind him, Muted meows come from him as he grimly hangs onto the stole with his teeth. He finds a quiet corner under the benches, starts arranging his prize on the floor and settles down on top of it and admires it.

Meanwhile, the bone thief is looking for a hiding place. The stairs seem to go up and up for a very long way. He sees some benches through a doorway and heads in that direction. He now hears feet coming up the stairs and looks for a dark corner. He curls up, drops the bone and inspects his prize.

The priest reaches the gallery, pauses for a good look around. Not seeing anything, he heads up to the bell-tower.

The thief picks up his prize and heads back down the stairs. He collects his ginger accomplice, and they sneak past the second priest checking the confessional on the other side of the church. They head into the robing room. The partially open window lets them squirm out and take off across the churchyard.

When they arrive at the gang's hideout, they enter, bearing their prizes. They make their way up the room and stand before the queen lounging on her bed. She gets up and comes down to inspect the items deposited in front of her. She pushes the bone around carefully, examining it.

"It's an old, smelly bone, why did you bring me this?"

"The humans seemed to greatly prize it and chased us trying to get it back," the black cat replies.

She sniffs, "It's still a smelly old bone, not worthy of a cat burglar at all."

The beautiful white cat turns to the chubby ginger who is sitting there vacantly staring into space. She admires the beautifully embroidered green stole, as do all the other female cats and it is taken to adorn the bed of the queen. The rest all head towards their beds against the walls,

The black cat picks up the rejected bone and heads out of the building. His tail droops, and his pace is slow.

At the church the following morning there is great rejoicing, the relic is found back on its cushion. It's described as another unexplained mystery.

Martial Days (Olivia Arieti)

"He's dead, doctor, you can take your gloves off," Gladys said firmly.

Edgar gazed at her; her coldness never stopped vexing him.

"Just the time for a cigarette and prepare the next, nurse," he replied and walked out.

The sight of the young soldiers dying one after the other and not being able to help them was devastating. Sure, that was the war and its bloody claims, but it was so unfair and he felt so useless he wished he had never enlisted. Better to have stayed at his town's hospital, at home, instead of crossing the ocean to find himself in a damned unit where the basic medical treatments were lacking and working conditions extreme; not to mention the bombs echoing over your head, a continuous reminder that you may not see the sun rise again. Thank goodness, he wasn't married nor engaged... yes, there was a half promise with Lilian... She was waiting for him and he liked her; sweet, caring, elegant, surely, a perfect wife, but there was something that was holding him back... Now that he was facing death and destruction day after day, he realised how his world was futile, meaningless, almost unreal. He despised his superficiality, his lack of sensitivity. Enrolling was the only good thing he did. Luckily, there was Gladys, the lovely nurse whose frosty glance wasn't enough to conceal the warmest heart. She joined the forces to find her husband, an army pilot who had suddenly

115

disappeared from all radars and now was probably lying unconscious in some camp hospital bed or dead on a forlorn field. Her love was stronger than the horrors of the war and with unflinching determination, she went on in her quest.

"The patient's ready," Gladys shouted.

Edgar put on his gloves, mask and started his job.

"Well, we've made it this time," he said with a tight smile, satisfied at winning one of his many daily battles.

"He looks like Brandon, just a little younger."

'Always on her mind,' he thought, annoyed.

"Is there a chance that a cup of coffee with me might blur your memory for a few minutes?" he smiled. "These past hours have been quite tough for both of us."

They spent lots of time together, having to work side by side all day long and when the bombing continued also during the night.

"Aren't you afraid we might get killed sooner or later?" he asked, sipping his coffee.

"A good chance to find out what happened to Brandon and perhaps, to meet him again."

Edgar remained silent. For the first time, he wished someone loved him as much. Neither Lilian nor any of the girls he had dated were like the peppy nurse.

Gladys was unique and, although her abrupt manners irritated him, he appreciated her efficiency and frankness. She exhorted the injured boys not to cry over themselves and seemed deprived of that maternal feeling that the wretched always sought in

116

those horrible moments. Whenever there was a dying soul though, she would sit by his side, hold his hand and like an angel brighten his last minutes with the sweetest smile. Then she would go out and burst into tears.

In those moments, Edgar wished he could hold her in his arms and promise that it would soon be all over, but telling such a big lie would have been stupid.

As a matter of fact, the war kept raging fiercely and their efforts to save or heal most often failed. Nevertheless, they fought all adversities together and never stopped doing their job to the utmost.

The doctor became aware that his interest for the nurse went beyond mere admiration... Could it be love?

No, that was not the case... Working so close and in such a tragic situation altered whatever feeling... nevertheless, he found himself thinking about her before falling asleep and waiting anxiously to see her again the following morning; by now, her icy glance made him shiver with desire.

He was surprised when one evening she said, "I like you a lot, doc; if I weren't married, I'd let myself go."

An alluring light brightened her eyes and her smile was inviting...

"You might be a widow by now," he replied and immediately regretted saying it.

No slap on his face hurt him more, not even his father's.

The following morning, with swollen eyes, she cried, "I hate you! You almost made me forget the dearest husband of all," and without another word, got down to work.

The thought that Gladys might have some feelings for him filled Edgar with joy, but at the same time, left him disconcerted. However could he compete with an invisible presence, perhaps, now nothing more than a beloved memory?

They realized they needed to talk the matter over, to clarify, to dig into their tormented hearts.

By coincidence, both had been dispatched to another hospital quite a few miles away. It was safer to travel by night.

Once the car had started, Edgar said, "I love you, Gladys, there's nothing I can do about it. You can't imagine how hard I tried to fight the feeling aware that you belong to another man, but it's just too strong, too overwhelming."

"If you love me, help me find Brandon," she said drily.

"I shall, but you must promise that if he should be dead, you'll become my wife."

She nodded slightly, but that was enough. The deal was made.

Then Edgar pulled over by a huge tree.

"Kiss me, dear, at least once before who knows what may happen to both of us," he implored and took her in his arms.

Her lips were burning more than fire and he saw all the stars above fall into the rusty old jeep and form a luminous halo around them.

The echo of distant bombardments increased their wantonness as they presumed it might have

118

been the only and certainly, the last abandonment they would allow. A consuming kiss wasn't enough.

"I'll never forgive myself," she uttered once back on the road, "and even if I should, Brandon will never do it."

"I would have gone on forever, darling," he said indifferent to what he considered her raving. He didn't give a damn about Brandon or her conflicts; he only cared for her, the most wonderful thing that had ever happened to him.

The secondary roads were bumpy and it started raining; both remained silent for the rest of the trip, Edgar overjoyed, Gladys overshadowed by regrets.

As soon as they arrived, they realized there wasn't much time for personal problems. Wounded men kept coming in one after the other, the medical supplies were getting scarcer and the bombardments heavier. Death had become more than a threat and fear and hopelessness overtook all spirits whether fighting on the fields or in hospitals.

When the enemy raids hit sooner than expected, all took shelter, but the bombs were many and myriads of shells fell upon them. One killed Gladys on the spot.

Despair was more intense than the horror of the war. Edgar kept vigil on the body day and night; the face was peaceful, just a bit surprised for such a blow. He wondered if she had met Brandon at last. Fits of jealousy couldn't be avoided.

His grief was such that he objected to her burial, unwilling to let her go. If possible, he would have followed her into that improvised grave in the improvised cemetery that one day would be covered

119

by uncouth vegetation and visited by rabid fowls only.

No matter the sympathy of his comrades and superiors, he felt a horrid void around him. Wherever he turned his eyes, he saw her and whatever nurse assisted him was called Gladys. 'Gladys, the gloves, Gladys, the forceps,' and so on. He simply couldn't go on without her so he had to pretend she was still by his side no matter how insane he looked.

Talking to her had become normal and it soon caused concern in the bystanders, in the officers, in the lieutenant who insisted he should take a two week leave.

While packing up, Gladys appeared before him.

"I'm coming with you, love, I have a leave too," and she put her skeleton arms around him.

"Gladys, honey, you're back," he mumbled without believing his own words.

"I need your help, doc... remember your promise?"

"So you haven't found him yet?"

"We're not free to roam around in the first days, but now it will be alright." Here she paused and sighed. "For a while at least, they won't let me hang out too long."

"I'm heading south, baby, want to spend some time by the sea, have to change scenery."

"It's fine with me, I'll see you there."

Before he could say anything, she had disappeared.

Edgar was as worried as scared. Had he gone mad? Maybe, his superior was right, the endless work at the hospital had exhausted him and the signs of a nervous breakdown were more than evident. Going on talking to her would take him straight to one of the hospital wards side by side with his own patients.

Even if it was deep winter, the weather was splendid, warm and sunny, and the remote little village apparently carved in the hills surrounding it, was the perfect corner to relax.

Edgar had just ordered his cappuccino when Gladys sat beside him.

"It can't be," he exclaimed.

The waiter turned round, "Everything alright, Sir?"

"No, err... I mean, yes, thank you."

"Why so surprised, hon? I told you I'd come with you."

Then she smiled, "I hope you still want me."

"Of course, I do, but you're a... a..."

"A ghost, no need to be afraid of saying that. It happens to everyone sooner or later."

Luckily, the waiter couldn't understand the conversation; besides, the officer wasn't the first fellow he'd seen talking to himself. His glances, however, disturbed Edgar who quickly paid for the drink and left, followed by Gladys's ghost.

"Let's walk along the sea, it's such a lovely day and the view is spectacular."

It was during the stroll that it happened. On the shore stood a woman with a toddler scampering in the sand and beside her was Brandon, his arm around her shoulders.

If Gladys hadn't been a spectre, she would have become one at once. Her eyes turned gelid, her face more cadaverous than it already was.

"Brandon," she cried, "what on earth are you doing with that woman and that kid?"

But Brandon didn't turn round; he moved closer to his partner and kissed her tenderly as though willing to point out his new status.

"I'm sorry, Gladys, terribly sorry," Edgar said.

Tears fell down her hollow cheeks.

"This is the price lots of women pay to the war; when it's not your body, it takes your heart."

Now she was sobbing on his shoulder that, despite the flow of tears, didn't get wet.

They remained watching the family for a long time.

"The child's beautiful," she admitted and started weeping again.

"Let's go, honey, no use going on hurting yourself."

Somehow he managed to take her away. He wondered if Brandon had noticed the wacky guy talking to himself.

Everything seemed absurd, ironic, but his heart was throbbing for real and Gladys was there... He had never stopped loving her and now was in love with her ghost; a most awkward situation that no psychiatrist would ever understand.

A week later, Gladys said, "I have to keep my promise, Edgar, I'll be your wife."

"What shall I do, find a priest and tell him I'm wedding a spirit?"

He took her clammy hands, kissed them and whispered, "We'll have to wait, darling."

"I've lost Brandon, but I won't lose you and that's final."

When Edgar returned to the hospital, he looked better. He had begun sleeping again and Gladys seemed to have disappeared. His love and grief for her loss were the same as before, but he was determined to keep her out of his thoughts. The dramatic reality of the war helped him. The end was near; the fighting got fiercer and death seemed to prevail among both sides alike.

The troops were sent home in late spring and he had been finally dismissed. He would work again at the town's hospital, start seeing his old friends and that's all; he wouldn't marry Lilian or anybody else, Gladys would be in his heart forever... but she couldn't know that.

At the last crossroad before reaching his house, a white lorry crashed into his car. Edgar died on the ambulance where a pretty nurse with wings was holding his hand.

"Don't be afraid, darling, we're heading up," Gladys whispered, "the priest is waiting for us and the angels are already singing the nuptial hymn."

The doctor who was assisting him, never figured out how a dead body's lips could curl into a smile.

Flesh and Wood (Ken L Jones)

Pilate's hands washed
Crowds that jeered
More agony
Than a just man
Should endure
Many believed
Few understood
Most only saw
Flesh and wood.

He walked briefly
Raised the dead
Told the infirm
To take up their beds
Fed the crowds
Calmed the storm
Stopped the hypocrite's
Flying stones.

Forgave the whore
And the man who taxed
Finally sponged off
Cain's bloody mark
Pitied those who
Should have understood
Because they only saw
Flesh and wood.

Some remember only your words
Some imperfectly mimic your deeds

Some wait for your return
While ignoring the world
Some use your name to
Justify their own needs.

Worst yet some chose
Not to remember you at all
Or only in times of trouble
Chose to call
Or deny when questioned
In a public place
Where they might be mocked
If your thirst they slake.

I have gathered your blood
In my splintered hands
To wash free my fears
And become your lamb
I am not perfect
Nor need to be
I've opened the door
To which you have extended
The key
I can now look beyond
Your agony
And see what was
Given birth to
On this section
of trees.

My questions have been answered
By my own belief
I now understand

My life time of grief
It's all so simple
Once it's understood
It's just a matter of
Being able to see
More flesh than wood.

Meet the Authors

Olivia Arieti lives in Torre del Lago Puccini, Italy, with her family. She writes drama, poetry and fiction. Her stories have appeared in several magazines and anthologies including, *Enchanted Conversations, Enchanted Tales Literary Magazine, Fantasia Divinity Magazine, Forgotten Tomb Press, Horrified Press, Infective Ink, Pandemonium Press, Sirens Call Publications, Blood Song Books, Black Hare Press, Pussy Magic Magazine, Stormy Island Publishing, Breaking Rules Publishing, Scarlet Leaf Review, Iron Faerie Publishing, Dark Dossier Magazine, Paramour Ink Press, Raven and Drake Publishing.*

Dorothy Davies is an editor, writer, and medium. Somehow all these things come together in her seemingly crowded leisure and work life. She retired from editing for a while to run a second hand shop, the best one on the Isle of Wight, but the thrill of finding and publishing outstanding stories became too much so she started again with the Gravestone Press imprint. She still runs the shop…Her book, The Skullface Chronicles, the story of a zombie taking revenge on his dysfunctional family, is available through fiction4all.com. She has a store of short stories, some of which are finding their way into the anthologies, having not seen daylight for many a long year. She also channels books from spirit authors, notable figures from our history. These can be found on the fiction4all.site under Zadkiel Publishing.

Shashi Kadapa, based in Pune, India, is the managing editor of ActiveMuse, a journal of literature. He is the 2021 International Fellow of the International Human Rights Foundation, NY. Thrice nominated for Pushcart Prize, he is a two-time award winner of the IHRAF, NY short story competition. Writing across various genres, his works have appeared or forthcoming in anthologies of parAbnormal, Casagrande Press, Anthroposphere (Oxford Climate Review), Alien Dimensions #11, Agorist Writers, Escaped Ink, War Monkey, Carpathia Publishing, Sirens Call Publications, Samie Sands, Mitzi Szerto, and others. Please follow these links to review his works: http://www.activemuse.org/Shashi/Shashi_Pubs.ht ml

Chris Marchant currently lives in the Normandy region of France with her partner and far too many cats. She writes mainly science fiction, fantasy and historical, but veers off course now and then. She is currently working on an historical Gamelit/LitRPG novel. Her website is www.chrismarchantwriter.com. She also has guardianship of #Drizztthemusecat.

Rickey Rivers Jr was born and raised in Alabama. He is a Best of the Net nominated writer and cancer survivor. His work has appeared in the JJ Outre

Review, Stellium Literary Magazine, Fabula Argentea (among other publications).

Rie Sheridan Rose multitasks. A lot. Her short stories appear in numerous anthologies, including Killing It Softly Vol. 1 & 2, Hides the Dark Tower, Dark Divinations and On Fire. She has authored twelve novels, six poetry chapbooks and lyrics for dozens of songs. She is also editor-in-chief for Mocha Memoirs Press and editor for the Thirteen O' Clock imprint of Horrified Press. She tweets as @RieSheridanRose.

E. S. Sibbald is a young writer working in the library and education industry. They remain alive only by devouring words and worlds. When not living in their own mind, they reside in Sydney, Australia. They can be found on twitter at @essibbald.

SJ Townend hopes that her stories take the reader on a journey to often a dark place and only sometimes back again.
SJ won the Secret Attic short story contest (Spring 2020), has had fiction published with Sledgehammer Lit Mag, Hash Journal, Ghost Orchid Press, Bandit Fiction, Black Hare Press, Black Petals Horror Magazine, Ellipsis Zine, Gravely Unusual, Gravestone Press, Holy Flea, Horla Horror and was long listed for the Women on Writing non-fiction contest in 2020.
She has also written and self-published two dark mystery novels, both of which are available to

purchase elsewhere: (Tabitha Fox Never Knocks, Twenty-Seven and the Unkindness of Crows).
Follow her on Twitter: @SJTownend